After struggling to discover his power, Abyss is tasked with an epic quest to seal the God of Fire, assisted with the immortal huntress Diana and many mysteries from the animal kingdom. Along the way, he meets the half-siblings Inder and Latis, while an ancient Pharaoh desires to mold the boy for devious purposes.

Abyss is caught up in the secret, hectic crossfire between the Witch-selected heroes and the golden-armored clerics, and unearths a strange diamond blade while defending himself from enemies. His action breaks the seal of the God of Fire, who threatens to throw the world into strife and chaos. As he journeys across the land to redeem himself, Abyss stumbles across many who would seek his power. A resurrected tribal warlord demands that Abyss follow his ancestors' path of war and conquest, while the Pharaoh's servant, Grigory, sees him as a tool to purify and strengthen humanity.

As he discovers his shortcomings and weaknesses in his perilous journey, many of his peers judge him to be incompetent and question fate itself. Plants, animals, and even space-time itself warp around Abyss as he continues to borrow animal parts from various species.

In spite of his enemies and doubters, Abyss continues to persevere in his quest. For no matter how chaotic and uncertain the future may seem, destiny is not something that merely calls, but is something that is to be forged.

Hero of the Abyss
Copyright © 2024 Andy Hsieh
ISBN: 978-1-4874-4030-5
Cover art by Martine Jardin

Published by eXtasy Books Inc

Look for us online at:
www.eXtasybooks.com

HERO OF THE ABYSS
JOURNEY INTO CHAOS 1

BY

ANDY HSIEH

DEDICATION

For aspiring young heroes all over the world.

CHAPTER ONE

The day I was hit by that truck was both the best and the worst day of my life. It was the day that I became a hero and started my story with all of its glory, tragedy, and unpleasant dirty tasks involved. To this day, I still have split thoughts on whether or not I should thank the Witch from the bottom of my heart or curse her until my throat runs hoarse and dry.

I started out life as an ordinary boy, living in prosperous first-world America within the even more comfortable suburbs. Of the eight billion people in a vast, unforgiving world, many would obviously envy being in such a position. But as I spent the last few days of my summer break before I entered eighth grade, I couldn't help but sigh in disappointment.

It probably wasn't uncommon for little kids to daydream of becoming a superhero. All it took was some radioactivity, a mutation, or discovering that one parent was a Greek god, right? I looked forward to the day that I could stretch my limbs and smash them like rubber, or when I could make thousands of screaming clones to fight evil villains with a stupid smile on my face. I supposed middle school was designed to be that difficult time where kids discovered that they had more academic responsibilities and had to get used to the boring parts of life. At one point in my life, I would have probably settled for playing basketball for a living, but as middle school went on, I'd continued to retain my short height while others started their growth spurts. I was good at dribbling and passing but wasn't a sharpshooter and lacked a fancy layup package, so there was probably no way I would've even made the high school team.

And so I began getting lost in books, comics, card games, and video games like I'd never even left elementary school. My parents had directed me to pay more attention to my studies recently, and my brother certainly complied. But I had at least one more year to go of middle school before I had things to worry about, right? I'd only turned thirteen a few weeks ago, after all. I imagined myself ten years in the future wiping potato chip crumbs off my face as yet another fat nerd in a comic book shop. The modern world was generous, and there were jobs for awkward geeks and man-children.

As I walked home from the library, once again a little disappointed at how cliché some of the novels I'd returned had ended up being, I saw a young girl walking across the street, probably no older than eight or nine. She had the right of way in the crosswalk but didn't see the truck that was roaring down the street.

Had its driver fallen asleep at the wheel in such broad daylight?

I acted without thinking, dropped my backpack, and rushed toward the girl. I hadn't intended to sacrifice myself, but I knew that if I really sprinted, I could take one of her arms and drag her out of harm's way. "Look out!" I yelled, and the girl turned in time to see the truck, freezing in her tracks. At that point, I realized I'd overestimated my own speed and that I would only reach the girl if I dove.

Time seemed to slow down then. As I collided full-force with that girl, my light frame ended up being enough to throw her out of harm's way, but now that I was stuck in a full dive, I'd made the unintended sacrifice. The truck didn't even honk. And by some odd miracle, its front bumper sent me flying upwards, spinning sideways as I heard my ribs crunch from the collision.

So at least I get a nice view of the sky and the distant mountains before I die, right?

As I floated helplessly in mid-air, I looked across all of the people on the street and in their cars. Would I be remembered as a hero? *Perhaps I, who had only been destined to be an underachieving geek, had saved the woman who would eventually cure cancer? Or perhaps I'd saved the next corrupt politician, and generations after would curse me for not letting the girl die.*

As I made another half-spin in my mid-air flight, I made eye contact with a teenage girl walking alongside the sidewalk with hazel hair and eyes. She was exotically beautiful with mixed-race features and seemed innocently concerned for pathetic old me trying to become a wannabe hero. And then I saw my memories start to flash before my eyes. It wasn't a bad last sight, laying my eyes on a pretty girl before I truly went into the inevitable, right?

Except that I didn't watch my memories alone. I felt this hazel-haired girl watching them alongside me, as if she was in the theater and I was on the stage. I saw all the times my brother beat me at video games and basketball, and how awkward I'd been in social interactions, wanting to shrink away from the world when I was bullied. And then she probably saw the stupid daydreams, the messy drawings that I made where I imagined I would one day be a hero. She saw how immature I was when I geeked out regarding *Magic – the Gathering* combos and strategies in video games and how my imagination and ambition were too powerful for this reality.

"The truck is the perfect way to go to another world in anime, right?"

I heard the words as a voice in my head. This was better than getting stabbed for sure, and if I just warped while I walked home from a convenience store, I wouldn't like my odds of living a happy life. *"If you can, hazel-haired girl, take me to another world,"* I begged as I looked at her with my anxious gaze. *"If you want to give me a second chance, let me also live a much more exciting life."* The girl didn't respond as I began the downward portion of my trajectory. I was probably just hal-lucinating things, but the ground looked like it was starting to rumble beneath me.

The last thing I saw before my eyes stopped working was an enormous fissure forming within the road and a pitch-black, rising column of oil shooting upwards to swallow me in jet-black darkness.

"His ribs and spine have almost all healed up now," I heard a girl's voice from above me. Was I in the hospital? I still felt pain in my right side where the truck had hit me, and as I tossed and turned and struggled to open my eyes, I discov-ered that I was indeed on a bed. "He's waking, finally!"

When I opened my eyes, I discovered that although I'd been resting on a bed, I wasn't in a hospital at all, but what appeared to be a small cabin. The girls and boys surrounding me weren't in medical outfits either, and I wasn't in a medical gown. However, someone had changed me into a brown tunic and a new set of shorts. "Where . . . where am I?" I asked. When I tried to sit up, I winced from the pain, and the girl watching over me gestured to a cup of lime juice sitting on the desk to my right.

"You're in the Western Sanctuary for the Witches' heroes," the girl explained as I took a sip of the juice. I wasn't sure if I heard her right, so I tried to repeat.

"I haven't ever heard of a hospital named Wi-chez-herus," I started. "Did I die in that collision with the truck? Am I in the afterlife?"

The girl shook her head. "Witches' heroes. Witches as in powerful female mages, heroes as in the ones that go on epic quests and battles." I chuckled at the absurdity of what she was saying. "This is no laughing matter. You were chosen by the most powerful Witch, and you made a contract to serve her . . ."

4

"Right, right," I muttered as I continued inspecting the cabin I was in. All I remembered while I was sailing through the air was locking gazes with that hazel-haired girl. "So this lime juice that I'm drinking, will it give me the special powers that I need on this quest?"

One of the boys sighed. He looked around sixteen and was tall, muscular, and handsome with red hair, but he had understanding green eyes. "He doesn't believe us. It could be that the legendary Witch didn't brief him during his contract." The red-headed boy disappeared from existence and popped up right next to me on the bed. I looked at the teleporting boy in shock for a few seconds, and then a stupid grin began to form on my face.

"So she chose an idiot to contract with as a hero, huh?" the girl asked, shaking her head. The red-haired boy demonstrated his power again after counting a few seconds silently and blinked back to my left side like a video game character.

"The news reports said that he dove head-first to save a little girl," the teleporting boy said. My grin grew wider and dumber, and I tried to cover my mouth. "That's the defining quality of a hero, not intelligence and strength. We can go over everything slowly. I'm Simon Williams, the leader of the heroes within this Western Sanctuary. The girl you're talking to is Ruth Gingerfield, and her power is being able to discover remedies for injuries like the lime juice you're drinking. When we got you here, though, you were already in surprisingly good condition. It was as if the oil pit that you landed in began working on your wounds and stopped the internal bleeding within your organs."

"So my power is related to . . . oil?" I muttered, scratching my head. I realized that I should begin to make my own introduction and found that I was missing one important piece. "Um, my name is Atom . . . Ano . . . Anon . . ."

"So her legendary magic applies to her hero, as well, does

it?" Simon shrugged. "The Witch that you made your contract with was given many countermeasures in order to protect her identity so that the priests and the hunters wouldn't be able to track her. She was supposed to be our trump card in case of any emergency, but I can't believe she made that contract with you without thinking. If you can't remember your name due to the magic protection, we can call you Abyss because you fell into the Abyss . . ."

"And because he's probably going to make an *abysmal* hero," one of the boys in the corner started. Simon teleported right up to him and slapped him across the face.

"Justin, don't interrupt while I'm briefing." Justin still had a smug smile on his face, as if he'd been fully prepared for such punishment as Simon walked back toward my position on the hospital bed. So it appeared that his teleportation had a cool-down period — even then, it was an awesome power, and I was glad that we had this guy on our side rather than having to deal with him as an enemy. But so many thoughts were whirring through my head, remembering the multitude of fantasy stories and shows that I'd read before. *Anyone could betray me in this moment, even if I'd managed to stumble across the lucky stars and discover a secret, magical world.*

"Abyss . . . Abyss isn't a bad name," I said, deciding. "Go on, Simon."

"A lot of us aren't so clear about why the world was like this in the first place," Simon began. "Perhaps we know less than scientists do regarding the laws of physics. But long ago, the God of Fire made a deal with human females. He would grant them magic to assist with their oath of trying to lead the world into a peaceful era, one with less death and suffering.

"Because the Witches themselves can't engage in violence, they made contracts with heroes like you and me in order to carry out their missions. Our main oppositions have always been, well, large organized religions, be it small groups of terrorists or large networks of priests. They believe that there's meaning in human suffering, in tragic death even, so they hunt down the Witches because they're suspicious that we might promise a false utopia."

I nodded.

"So it's not quite as convenient as you might expect," Simon said. "Heroes are mostly manned for defense or gathering supplies for the sanctuary as we try to get closer and closer to the Witches' goals of peace. It's not like there are villains for us to fight or monsters for us to kill."

"How do I discover what my power is?" I asked as I stood up and brushed off my blankets.

Simon sighed. "Usually it's simple, where the hero inherits the power that the Witch was granted with. But in your case, we don't even know if the legendary Witch would be able to bestow her hero with proper powers without making him . . . well, explode. Perhaps you'll discover your power in times of need."

As I stretched and started pacing around the room, I didn't notice anything particularly different from my body.

"But general combat training helps everybody, so perhaps you can start there."

"Can't I just ask this legendary Witch exactly what she gave me?" I asked. I was getting irritated by having to call her that. "How about we call her Lime?" I jested, thinking of the lime juice that Ruth had prepared me. "Or Time, or Grime, or Dime?"

No one laughed, and I could tell that Justin was trying to hide a sneer. So, even when taken to a magical place, my sense of humor and social skills remained as poor as ever. Regardless, I was still excited that I was able to go on this new adventure. Even if things wouldn't be as convenient as a video game or novel, it meant being able to explore a world full of magic and possibility. If I'd wanted to explore the mundane world, I would have the risk of being eaten by a tiger or bit by a venomous snake, and I probably wasn't smart or physically fit enough to become an astronaut.

"It's best not to make contact with her," Simon said. "Her existence must remain as much a secret as possible, and if she meets you, it may trigger her own self-destructive potential." How conveniently ominous.

The Western Sanctuary appeared rather small, perhaps containing fewer buildings than the middle school I attended. It was situated in a narrow valley with a mysterious forest at all sides, and Simon led me down toward the training fields. "What about my parents, my family?" I suddenly wondered.

"We have a Witch who's able to create the illusions of absent heroes who are working in the sanctuary," Simon explained. "You'll get to go back to them sooner or later, depending on how things play out here."

I discovered that most of the people in this camp were boys or young men. After looking in the bathroom mirror, I was upset that I retained my short height and plain appearance with my scruffy black hair. I had thought that contracting with the Witch would at least make me more muscular or change my eye color if I didn't get any taller.

In the training grounds below, most of the heroes fought with wooden spears and swords, although some of them preferred to fight bare-handed, which was perhaps more conducive to the magic that their Witch granted them.

"If we're lucky, you'll be able to discover your power while you sharpen your combat skills down there, and we can kill two birds with one stone."

I nodded to Simon with an enthusiastic smile and headed toward the sword-fighting arena first. Everyone was given a simple wooden sword. Although they seemed rather plain, the fighters definitely seemed more intensely motivated than any time that I'd spent fighting with sticks as a kid.

I grabbed onto a sword and didn't feel any magic running through my veins, and I soon approached the crowd of boys who were training. "Uh . . . I'm Abyss," I started. "It's nice to meet all of you."

Simon took over from there. "Abyss needs help discovering his power, as he made his contract with the legendary Witch, she who should not be named. Make sure you teach him everything you know about combat."

None of the boys seemed excited to train me, so I started doing some simple practice swings and stabs as I watched the others duel.

Eventually, one of them walked up to me and tapped me gently with his sword. "Someone's got to try sparring with the newbie, right?"

"Thanks," I started softly, and I expected to get beaten down until I could figure out what my power was. But surprisingly enough, the first thirty seconds of the duel went better than I imagined. I was blocking and parrying most of my challenger's strikes, almost as if I knew where he was swinging ahead of time.

He didn't show frustration, looking rather satisfied that I could hold on for so long.

Smack!

And then, after that short thirty-second period, I began getting clobbered by the sword, racking up new bruises to my healing abdomen and my arms. All of a sudden, I wasn't holding up with my defense, and soon, I fell over to the ground in embarrassment.

"What was that?" the boy said as he offered me a hand and helped me up. "When we started, it was almost as if you've at least had a couple of years of regular sword training, and then you went limp and let yourself get hit everywhere."

I shrugged. "I have no idea either."

Some of the other boys took interest and weren't shy about expressing their quick initial judgments.

"Maybe Simon and the others brought in a poor contract," they muttered. "Was this guy just chosen because he got run over by a truck?"

"Let's go again." I turned to the boy who'd approached me. So it was a rough start, just like every good old underdog story in the world. "I'm sure I can figure out my power somehow."

"Sure," the boy said, showing me his friendly blue eyes. "I'm Hugh Larhouse, by the way."

In my second spar with Hugh, I tried to use my thirty-second window of good swordsmanship to land aggressive attacks, but apparently, the skill I'd mustered only applied to my defense.

Hugh could see my wide and clumsy swings and could do anything when responding to one of my offensive maneuvers. My whole body was left open when I attacked, and if I tried to dodge his sword strike, he could go for a low kick or a front kick and add more purple bruises to my frame.

"Heh . . . " I started, panting for breath as I propped myself up from the ground after our fifth duel. Hugh was quickly getting bored of sparring with me, however, and turned to the other boys.

"I'll find out my magic soon," I said to myself, but anyone who heard my announcement didn't seem to believe it. I went to every sword-wielder willing to train with me, and the results were the same as they'd been with Hugh. I could hold up with my defense alone for twenty or thirty seconds before getting clobbered by a barrage of sword strikes.

After a couple of hours, my body was aching, and I wondered if I would have better luck when it came to spears or fighting bare-handed.

It was the same result with the spears, as if the Witch that had contracted with me was mocking me. I headed over to the boxers, trying to give it one last chance, and by then, everyone had heard of my initial failures. Very few people even considered boxing with me. The Witch, who should not be named, had wasted her magical contract on a short, awkward loser like me instead of choosing a proper hero—that was the conclusion that most of the heroes in this sanctuary had come to.

"I'll spar with you," a racially ambiguous boy with brown skin volunteered. He was a good few inches taller than me like everyone else, and his curly black hair was far less scruffy than mine. He had both confidence and intelligence in his eyes, something that I was never really able to display as the awkward, geeky student.

I quickly shook myself out of my slump and forced my tired body to start boxing with him.

"Go easy on him, Sonny."

Some of the boys decided to watch the Witches' prime failure, perhaps to make them feel better about themselves.

Sonny raised an eyebrow, and I shook my head.

"Show me all you've got," I decided. "Maybe I really need to be pushed to the edge to awaken my power."

"Ruth will be quite upset if we force her to make more healing potions," Sonny said. "But I like your style." Sonny held out a fist, and I tapped it without hesitation, ready for another round of bruises.

How long would I last? Sonny appeared to be an out-boxer and quickly shuffled his feet. He used his longer limbs to dance circles around me and pummeled at my defenses. Again, the same phenomenon was happening. My defense, and only my defense, was good for thirty seconds, as my arms reacted on their own to block Sonny's quick barrage of punches.

Sonny seemed quite amused and smiled, but the boys watching the fight began to jeer.

"He's the thirty-second turtle!" One of them claimed.

"You going to counter?" Sonny asked.

I knew that the moment I tried to counter would be the moment I would need several stitches in the face and lose a couple of teeth. But my thirty seconds of good defense were going to run up, and I felt like merely blocking would make me look even weaker. My arms were sore from smacks from swords, spears, and now Sonny's devastating flurry of jabs, but I was sure that I could manage a punch.

"Living things evolve," Sonny started. "Perhaps one day, a turtle can evolve into a ferocious velociraptor. Let's evolve, Abyss!"

Sonny might have been counting thirty seconds in his head as he reached out for a real punch now, pushing off his back leg—it wasn't merely a jab this time. I was sure that I was going to have my nose crushed in, but I weaved to the left, perhaps dodging Sonny's knuckles by half a centimeter. And now was my opening. Sonny's chin was left unguarded, and if I just gave him a strong uppercut . . .

It felt like I hurt my knuckles more than I hurt Sonny's chin. Immediately after my blow connected, Sonny followed up with a left punch, hitting me straight in the gut, and I keeled over from the impact.

"*Retcch*!" I groaned, the air popping from my lungs. He followed up by smashing in my cheek, although I felt like he was holding back compared to the blow in my stomach. I toppled over as my vision went black, and I didn't think I could get up in less than ten seconds.

And now the boys started their oh-so-necessary commentary. "Sonny, you let him hit you on purpose, didn't you?"

"That might've been the weakest uppercut I've ever seen. He didn't have proper footwork or anything."

"Maybe the Witch, who should not be named, just sent us some comic relief to reward us for our hard work." It might have been fifteen or twenty seconds, but the darkness and pain eventually faded from my vision, and I forced myself up to my feet.

"Let's go again . . . " I croaked, not caring how pathetic I looked. I wasn't going to let this new opportunity in life go to waste. I knew that playing basketball for a living or becoming a successful inventor or scientist was way out of my potential, but I was going to do my best now that I'd entered this world of magic, even if all I could do was delay a major antagonist for a while. If I couldn't be a main character, I wouldn't settle for being the comic relief.

Sonny raised an eyebrow and looked around to see the other boys were shaking their heads.

"Give up on him," I recognized that Justin, the boy who had eagerly predicted that I'd be an abysmal hero, had now come over to witness the spectacle.

Sonny then looked back at me. "Are you serious about improving?" I nodded, and Sonny chuckled a bit. "Justin, even if he doesn't become a proper hero, I can't turn down an aspiring boxer."

"This isn't a sports camp." Justin rolled his eyes. "Simon's generous and says that we can wait a few days, maybe even a week, to see his power. But I'm saying the Witch wasted her contract and that it would be better to just approach her and suggest a replacement. The boy should consider himself lucky he survived getting hit by a truck."

Sonny put a hand on my shoulder. "Anyone who risks his life to help a fellow human is worthy of being my friend, and I'll stand up for him. Your counterattack and uppercut shows promise, but you just need more training and work."

"It didn't look like I dealt any damage to you at all," I said.

"I have a strong jaw since I've been boxing all my life." Sonny grinned. "Well, as long as I could walk and talk, I mean."

None of the other boys were really eager to train me in boxing compared with Sonny, so I spent the rest of the day boxing with him. I never managed to land another hit on him, and my mysterious power didn't awaken either.

When it came time to have dinner in the cafeteria, Sonny invited me to his seat, and I was surprised to see that he usually sat alone. He ate a pretty big meal to reflect the calories he burned as a boxing enthusiast, and I was also famished. I gulped down mashed potatoes and whatever meat that this Western Sanctuary was serving.

"May I ask what your power is and how you contracted with your Witch?" I asked.

Sonny chuckled. "It's nothing special. My power is lame compared to Simon's, you see. I met my patron Witch when I was cleaning up trash on the highways, just doing some volunteer work for my school. There was a huge car accident nearby, and I rushed forward and tried to budge the door to free the people trapped within. When a nearby Witch noticed my struggle, she granted me my power. It's really simple. I can power-up my physical strength for one to five minutes a day, depending on its magnitude, or if we're dealing with super-reinforced magical armor or barriers, I can send all my energy into a punch to channel tons of force. But the recoil hits my muscles really hard, and even after I go to sleep, usually Ruth has to brew healing potions."

"And how long have you been under contract?" I asked.

"Around three years, so I don't think my glass-cannon problem will go away anytime soon," Sonny said. "And honestly . . . I'm sort of disappointed at how the Western Sanctuary still can't be called my friends. Maybe I can only make friends with awkward losers and blind people." Sonny didn't seem to mind that I was included in the former category and went on. "From the beginning, most of my extended family didn't approve of my existence. If you were wondering, I'm half-white, a quarter black, and a quarter Korean. But all that makes me is ethnically ambiguous rather than exotically handsome, right?"

"Well, you've got boxing going for you," I said. "A short, dorky kid like me could only function as an anime protagonist." A silence passed between us, and I tried to think of better jokes.

"I'm sure the Witch didn't just choose you as a joke," Sonny said.

"She might've chosen me as the first sacrificial pawn in her elaborate chess game then," I said. "Although that means if I'm lucky enough, I can become a queen if I reach the other side of the board, right?"

The following few days, I would try my hand at swordplay and spear fighting for maybe an hour before heading over to the boxers' arena with Sonny. He was the only one who I could truly call my friend in this mysterious sanctuary, but I'd never really desired popularity in the first place. Sonny taught me the basics of boxing and guided me in building leg strength and footwork in order to maximize the strength of my punches and effectively bob and weave out of harm's way. However, during my lunch breaks or whenever I felt bored, I would wander on the outskirts of the camp and try anything and everything to channel the magic that the Witch had granted me.

"Water!" I yelled near the birdbath, trying to summon even a little trickle of water into my hands. "Come, wawawa . . . water!" I didn't care if I looked like an idiot. "Poseidon, water, please?"

Other times, I would head over to the forge where the crafting heroes were creating their actual weapons, shaping the molten steel diligently with their hammers. "Fire! Vulcan, Hephaestus, bring me the breath of a happy dragon!" I tried to spew a column of flame from my mouth.

"Wind! Wind, stormy winds here . . . " I started and spun

around like a moron trying to create any semblance of a mini-tornado. I also tried to spin a ball of air in my hands and gently bend the air to no avail. I became very dizzy afterward on my way back to sparring with Sonny.

"That just leaves Earth. Well, maybe light and shadow, too." But I was in contact with the earth at all times, and it never helped me in my spars against Sonny. If I could, I would settle with using the earth to trip Justin as he jeered at me. No matter how I stomped the ground, it wouldn't shake one bit.

On my fourth day since I'd entered the Western Sanctuary, Simon approached me as I was eating breakfast along with Sonny. "You spend most of the day training, and you've got the attitude for it, that's for sure," Simon began. "But a lot of us can't help that the contract you made really was a mistake." I looked away in frustration and soon realized that Sonny wasn't going to jump through hoops to stand up for me.

I turned back to Simon. "I've learned a lot about boxing from Sonny, and I'm only going to get better from here. Even if my power never awakens, I'll prove to all of you that I can become a hero, even if I just have my four limbs." Simon looked at me as if he was a parent trying to be patient with an unruly child. "Why don't we settle this right now? Your teleportation magic is fancy, but nothing I can't handle. If I beat you in a boxing match, you'll have to accept me as a hero worthy of this sanctuary. If I lose, you can kick me out or whatever . . ."

"Abyss, don't!" Sonny began, but it was too late. That was when magic pulsed through the air and surrounded Simon and me in a cloud of red runes.

"The wager is sealed," I heard Justin's voice as he stepped into the room with his familiar sneer. So that was why he acted so arrogant. I'd walked right into the trap of a hero who had the ability to bait out displays of confidence and then use those words to magically ensure that certain conclusions would occur. Even if Justin couldn't use his magic for combat, he was certainly a valuable ally when it came to outwitting the enemy or getting rid of problematic or useless allies.

"You have ten minutes to finish your breakfast," Simon said. "After that, you will meet me in the boxing fields, and we will settle this according to Justin's seal. I will warn you that even if you awaken your power, you have little chance of beating me in a serious fight. We'll have to see what power the legendary Witch has decided to grant you." I wanted to hope that Simon was only doing this in hopes that my power would be forced out, but I also knew that he probably wouldn't go out of the way to deal with Justin's seal.

"Any tips?" I asked Sonny as I finished the remains of my breakfast. Sonny could only shake his head with a sullen expression.

"Simon's good at boxing even without using his magic," Sonny said. "If your magic can extend to mind-reading with that tough defense that you showed, you might be able to surprise him when he teleports."

"Let's hope for that," I said as I headed over to the boxing fields. A small crowd of a dozen or so boys and girls were gathered around to watch the fight, and I warmed up a little, bouncing from side to side on my feet. When Simon came and entered the fray, I was not only reminded of my short height, but also impressed by how tall and muscular he was. He was at least nine inches taller than me with longer limbs, perhaps a couple of inches taller than the average man standing above six feet.

"Enthusiasm isn't enough to be a hero," Simon began. "But I might as well see what Sonny's taught you." As Simon began with simple footwork and jabs, I wondered if this was perhaps my only chance to defeat him. When I tried to press the offense, however, I noticed that Sonny had properly warned me. Getting close enough to Simon to hit him seemed impossible with how short my limbs were, and if I tried to rush in and overextend, he could easily respond by smashing in my nose. Simon tried not to show his disappointment, but I could sense boredom in his eyes.

I gritted my teeth. "Why don't you start teleporting already?" Another punch of mine was swiftly parried by Simon's left arm.

"Simon, he's asking for it," Justin began. "Show him your combo strings."

Simon shifted his feet silently and began pressing the offense. His jabs came out faster and stronger now. I blocked two of his punches, but the third hit me straight in the gut, and I bit down the pain, knowing that this would probably be when he was going to teleport. I jumped to the side, but Simon continued to press forward without using his magic. By a miracle, I managed to parry his fourth punch and had a blocking arm ready when he started his fifth . . .

"Agh!" I groaned as I fell forward and stumbled down. Simon had teleported behind me mid-punch and had preserved his body's motion to hit me in the back before I could react.

"He's down!" the boys cheered, and they started counting. A swarm of frustrating memories flooded into my mind. So would this be another story of how pathetic I was? Even when I was lucky enough to make it into this secret world of Witches and heroes, I wouldn't be able to prove my worth. I remembered all of the times I played basketball—even if I wasn't the worst player on the team, I was useless, and there had been nothing I could do to help my team even make the game close when it came to blowouts. Some opposing guards would pop up for a deep jumper in front of my face, while others would blow by me and force our predictable zone defense to collapse. When I tried to cut to the corners and shooting, the ball would just rim out, and even if I managed to cross-over a slower guard, the opposing center would be ready to swat away my shot at the rim. The best I could do was take charges on defense or pretend I was fouled.

"Five . . . six . . . " What was I even thinking? This was my last chance to escape a predictable, boring adult life, and I wouldn't give it up. I wanted to see more magic and go beyond seeing Simon beat me up while teleporting. There might be princesses out there waiting to be saved, and besides, I didn't want to waste the training that Sonny had given me. I struggled to my feet and forced a grin up at Simon, raising my guard once more.

"Not bad," I said, and Simon still looked at me with a disappointed sigh.

"Abyss, I heard you came from a well-off family. Maybe you could just find your place in boxing and wrestling." Simon didn't seem to be joking as he readied his fighting stance once more. His teleportation would be off cool-down soon, but I also knew that he wouldn't be hasty when it came to using it. I had to make a perfect prediction and hit Simon right as he teleported, just as Sonny suggested.

When Simon pushed the offense again, however, I didn't have time to guess. He was a blur of fists in front of me, and the best I could do was slightly bruise his forearms as he showed both his boxing prowess and his natural size advantage through the next couple of minutes. I was going to spend the next morning with bruises all over my chest and a couple on my cheeks, but I wanted to push whatever magic the Witch gave me to its fullest potential. When Simon hit me with a hard right, I blocked and stumbled backward, and that was when I noticed that he was slowing down.

It was an obvious feint, the wide haymaker that only amateurs would use when any street fighter could disrupt with a simple jab. He was going to settle it by showing off his teleportation magic once again, mixing it in with an attack that was too slow to work from the front. I swung around and punched, expecting to connect with something—anything, and only managed to hit air. I must have looked like a complete idiot and anticipated laughter as I turned around once more to face Simon.

Before I could meet his eyes, Simon had me way up in the air by one of the arms and slammed me down into the hard ground face-first. The spectators broke into raucous laughter as I heard them start the countdown—the countdown to the last seconds I could enjoy in this new world of Witches and heroes.

I began breaking down and crying as I realized that the shock from the slam made it impossible for me to get up in a minute, let alone ten seconds. The best I could do was pound my fist a little at the dirt in futility and curse at the hazel-haired girl who had saved me. "Are you enjoying this now, Witch?"

"Seven . . . eight . . . " Simon must have really slammed me down hard, for I realized that I was hearing a mysterious rumbling in the ground yet again. It was as if the story of Daedalus' labyrinth was true, and something was working its way up into the world from underground. "Nine . . . ten! He's out!" Well, whatever was moving down there, it didn't come up fast enough to save me in this fight against Simon.

"Clerics! What are they doing here?" Simon exclaimed, and I felt a hand tug me to my feet. When I opened my eyes, I found that the entire Western Sanctuary was in chaos. An army of men in gold and white armor were accompanied by priests in similarly fashioned robes. I blinked for a bit too long to make sure that I wasn't hallucinating.

"We've got the leader!" one of the clerics yelled. When I opened my eyes, I saw that Simon was trapped against three opponents in a magical ring, unable to assist or receive assistance in his battle against his foes. I could see that he could still use his teleportation within the limits of the ring and was fighting the best he could with a sword that he had somehow drawn from his clothing.

"Winds," I heard Justin begin. "When it comes to west, north, south, and east, which of them all favors men the least . . . " Justin's incantation was cut off by a blast of air straight within his mouth, which robbed him of his vocal ability.

I could still see that his incantation had stirred up some winds around his feet, but the clerics had him subdued and hand-cuffed. "We have both the leader of this sanctuary and the second-in-command. The rest should be easy pickings."

"We're in a lot of trouble," Sonny said to me, still annoyed that he had to support my weight. "This would be a good time to activate any of the magic you received from the legendary Witch, Abyss. I could activate mine, but it won't be a pretty sight."

"The Witch, who shall not be named, has chosen her hero, I heard," one of the leaders of the clerics began. He was a tall blond man with blue eyes and wielded a golden staff in his hands. Part of his armor seemed to be broken off around his right shoulder, as if it had been tainted with a curse from an earlier battle, and he wore a scar under his right cheek. "She disguises his magic trail well, but I see and smell all evil." The staff-wielder pointed his staff over to me. "Perhaps a good choice to disguise it in such an unassuming, pathetic boy as well."

Well, the good news was that I had some magical ability after all. The bad news was that whatever power I wielded might be stomped out or stolen before my journey could even begin. Sonny shrugged me off, and I stumbled a bit as I tried to regain my footing. "You're not going to fight for me, are you?" I asked.

"You were chosen by the legendary Witch," Sonny began. "I was only granted simple power-up magic."

"Lord Melosh, no need to dirty your hands with this small fry." Two other clerics joined the staff-wielder's side as they eyed Sonny.

"I can at least take two of you clerics down," Sonny began as he worked his magic. He only got slightly more muscular, but uncomfortable-looking veins bulged from his arms and probably his legs as well from under his jeans. "And maybe I'll make another dent in your fancy armor, Melosh."

Melosh appeared to be content to watch as Sonny engaged his two subordinates, while I was still exhausted from losing the fight against Simon. And I watched in awe as Sonny quickly started punching in the two clerics. Even though it was two-on-one and the clerics were equipped with swords, the weapons only made light cuts in Sonny's skin as his punches and kicks started creating dents and cracks within the clerics' golden armor. The sheer shock from Sonny's punches was enough to take out the two underlings. Melosh shook his head as Sonny stood victorious, his attention mostly on me. No one else seemed eager to defend me, and if I tried to run, there was a good chance I would only encounter more chaos in the clerics' invasion.

"I'm far more disappointed with my underlings than impressed by you, Sonny," Melosh said as he stepped forwards. I felt like I blinked and missed another important piece as I saw Melosh's staff snap back like a whip, and a large bloody gash in Sonny's side suddenly appeared. "But I've seen your improvement, as basic as the magic you were granted was. That would have cut open an ordinary man."

"Sonny, that's enough," I started. "If they're here for me, no need to sacrifice yourself." Again, I heard the underground click through my feet. Whatever was making its way up through the earth better make it in time before Sonny bled to death from staff strikes.

"Don't underestimate what you can do," Sonny said softly. "You showed a lot of grit in training and against Simon . . ."

"What a motivational speech," Melosh said as his staff left another nasty gash on Sonny's abdomen and then another. "Oh my, you're losing composure."

Sonny sunk to his knees from pain as his blood began to dye the earth red. I took a step forward, my entire body still sore. Somehow, Sonny forced himself back up to his feet and roared back for one last final punch.

"Let's see your ultimate move," Melosh said as he gripped his staff.

Clink. That was the soft noise that Sonny's punch made when it hit Melosh's golden staff. It hadn't even left a scratch on the weapon. Melosh seemed disappointed as Sonny sunk down once more. Blood continued to trail from his wounds.

"Why?" I muttered as Melosh spun his staff and swung it underhand like he was playing golf. Sonny hurtled back several meters and smashed into the nearest tree, and I backed away as I looked at Melosh.

The rumbling in the earth grew louder and louder, and I began to hear a cacophony of voices. No, not only voices but also guttural groans and shouts from cavemen and our ape ancestors. Sonny's voice was intermixed amongst them, and I felt the muscles in my right arm begin to burn and twist as if being chopped into pieces by a master chef and then sewn together by hundreds of factory workers again and again. It was as if new bodies, new souls were living within my arm and being gathered into a single channel by this mysterious magic. A brilliant crystal blade sprouted from the ground, its hilt up to greet my inflamed right arm. I took the blade without hesitation and turned over to Melosh.

Before I could strike Melosh, he'd used his pole to vault backward several meters. "The diamond blade has resurfaced! Whoever can capture it will be promoted to bishop and be given a chance to become Grand Bishop!"

And with that, all of the remaining clerics had turned their eyes on me. *"That's* more like it!" I shouted. The next few minutes were a blur, but I felt the raw thrill that I'd always desired when I'd daydreamed about being a hero. My right arm moved like a ravenous monster, and as it sought out clerics left and right, I chewed through them with the diamond blade that I was now wielding. The blade and my arm were dragging the rest of my body in wild, unnatural motions, threatening to snap out of my socket as I stumbled along my two feet. Thankfully, the clerics didn't seem to reside in human bodies, and although my blade lopped off limbs and made deadly stabs here and there, reddish-orange, swirling gas would flow from the wounds instead of splattering blood.

This was my redemption amongst the Witches' heroes, finally!

I tried to remain optimistic as my shoulder muscles accumulated bruises and internal bleeding as the diamond blade dragged me left and right.

"He's unleashed! Lord, have mercy, the pagan gods!" one of the clerics exclaimed as he dropped his weapon and began praying somberly.

"So you're the real deal, huh?" Melosh began as he vaulted back up to me with his golden staff. And then, all of a sudden, the diamond blade was less aggressive on autopilot, as if it realized it was dealing with a powerful opponent. "It's still magic that none of us clerics and hunters have seen before, but that power and that blade you summoned will be ours."

"I don't think so," I yelled as I rushed forward with the diamond blade. Melosh blocked the five strikes I managed to launch. The cleric deftly adjusted his position along with his golden staff. He seemed frustrated that he had limited opportunities to retaliate, but he seemed to settle for kicking me in the stomach, which fortunately wasn't as brutal as getting whipped like Sonny had been. The diamond blade jerked me forwards once more, but this time, it was too rough and wriggled out of my hands and started digging back into the earth. "What gives? Hey!"

"So it was only temporary, but it was longer and farther than most have managed to make the blade budge," Melosh said as he stood over me. I grabbed at the blade's hilt and tried to yank it upwards, but both the sword and the earth seemed to have a differing opinion, and my new weapon disappeared back into the depths of the earth. "I want to gamble with your power, but it's dangerous. But if your basic magical code is the same, my staff can siphon some of your power . . ."

Thunk. An arrow stuck out right from Melosh's right shoulder where his armor was damaged. Melosh gritted his teeth and deflected the next arrow with his staff. "You even have the curse of the immortal hunter on you now," Mclosh said to me. "Consider yourself lucky, lad." The cleric decided that he couldn't complete his objective with his fresh wound and the mysterious archer hiding amongst the trees, and he vaulted backward with his staff once more, disappearing from my vision in just a few leaps.

As I looked around at the surroundings, I saw that Simon was dealing with the last of his three captors, and when he defeated the cleric, the magical ring he'd been trapped in dissipated. However, more eyes were on me than on him, though, having seen that I'd saved everyone with my diamond blade.

"So I'm useful after all, right?" I asked. My right arm and shoulder socket were still throbbing from being dragged around like a puppet from the diamond blade.

"Abyss, you pulled out the blade from underground, didn't you?" Simon asked as he walked up to me. For some reason, the glances of my peers seemed more fearful than appreciative.

"It was the only thing that I could use to fight against

Melosh," I started. "And it decided to dig back underground right in the middle of fighting him, so some archer saved me . . ."

A girl with short black hair and a bow in her hands emerged from the forest leaves and looked at us all with cold eyes. "So it ends up being a spoiled prince that pulls out the diamond blade, huh? Looks like I've got another troublesome hero to train."

CHAPTER TWO

"Spoiled prince?" I asked the girl. I was yet again thrust into confusion as the girl approached me. She had light brown skin and wore a brown tunic adorned with pelts of animal fur, thin ropes, and some decorative leaves. She wore a golden ribbon in her hair and a golden band on her arm. Those ornaments broke the rest of her outfit, which showed that she was a wild hunter. This archer would be considered beautiful if she wasn't on the skinny side and if she didn't have black marks on her cheeks like a cheetah. "Wait, so am I descended from a king after all?"

"Well, I've trained more than my fair share of idiots," the archer continued. Fortunately, Simon stepped forward to clear everything up. But unfortunately, he still wasn't here to deliver any good news.

"Justin's seal cannot be undone," Simon began. "You lost in the boxing match we participated in, so you can no longer stay at the Western Sanctuary. But before you leave, I can explain the problem with you pulling out the diamond blade, even if it did help us turn the tides of battle. A lot of heroes and Witches alike hoped that the diamond blade was just a myth, a legend, but now that it's shown up in the flesh, it's very bad news. The God of Fire was the one to grant Witches their power, but no one, not even he, can understand his intents."

"So he's crazy, like a Greek god who gets drunk and violent?" I asked.

Simon shook his head. "We call him a god because of lack

of terminology, but he represents the abstraction of chaos more. He's only kept in check by other forces that regulate natural laws and order, and if he was truly unleashed, well . . . the dead would spring back to life, and past and future events would merge, and we might even import all sorts of deadly landscapes and life forms from across the galaxy. In any case, the diamond blade was wielded by a legendary hero who fought against the excesses of the God of Fire and sealed away his ability to disrupt the flow of life and death. As long as it remained embedded within the earth, the God of Fire would have limited influence over this world." I then turned to the archer girl with the short black hair.

"Heh. I wonder if you'll create your greatest tragedy yet, Diana." Justin had recovered from the clerics' attempts to seal his voice as he turned to me. "Serves him right for pulling out the diamond blade."

I sighed. So for me, either the rough start to my hero's journey would continue, or I would be pushed into my tragic backstory for when I became the evil villain later on. "Well, Diana," I started. "I hope that you can help me on this quest to . . . return the diamond blade to its original position or whatever. You certainly saved my skin when I was fighting against Melosh."

Diana looked me up and down again. "As soon as I fulfill the terms of my contract, I'll be done with you, and you can find some other sucker to help you on your quest." I wasn't used to dealing with this sort of attitude. Even if I couldn't end up saving a princess, I wanted the first female to journey with me to at least be a little friendlier.

"Good luck on your quest," Simon said. Now that Sonny was injured, the tall redhead was the only one in this sanctuary to care about me. "We'll get you more fitting clothes and gear, but can't promise you much else."

As Simon led me over to one of the cabins, I tried to think

of better ways to break the ice with Diana. But I was never good at interacting with the opposite gender, or even the popular boys who knew that they were more athletic, funnier, or smarter than me. The clothing was surprisingly plain—I suited up in a white toga-like robe tucked in by a belt, wearing brown, reinforced under-armor beneath. I was equipped with a new set of shorts, and sandals replaced my plain sneakers. Supposedly, these clothes were more durable, as I probably wouldn't be able to pack much more than I could carry. As I looked in the mirror, I noticed three triangle-shaped scars had formed under my left eye, giving me a distinctive new look. There were similarly shaped scars forming on my neck. I imagined myself on the front of a comic book cover now and wondered if I would look better if I just further scarred underneath my eye with a knife. I chuckled to myself, nervous and excited for the new journey with Diana.

"Will Sonny be all right?" I asked Simon. "He really threw himself in harm's way to protect me, and I wished that diamond blade had come up sooner."

"Ruth says he'll make a full recovery," Simon answered. "But I would be more worried about myself if I was you. Diana helps heroes train and occasionally even assists them in their adventures, but every hero who trained under her has died a tragic death. Many say it's just a part of her curse, as she acquired her powers through unnatural means. But she can't reject her obligation to assist heroes, and neither can the heroes run from her. She claims to have been around for at least four thousand years, but no one can verify her immortality."

"Ah," I said. Diana didn't look any older than I was, but that might explain her bored attitude and probably also explain why she called me a prince. Perhaps she was distancing herself from me so that she wouldn't feel upset when I died. "So where can I find a map to where I can properly bury the diamond blade?"

"You won't," Simon answered. "The power you got from contracting with the Witch should guide you on your quest." It seemed that this was the final question Simon was in the mood to answer, for he turned away from me and attended to other matters as leader of this Western Sanctuary. He didn't seem to regret humiliating me in front of the crowd and seemed to be sure that the future chaos I ensured by pulling out the diamond blade would do more harm than the destruction I'd prevented by fighting for everyone's sake.

Diana was still waiting for me outside the cabin and gave me a simple command and gesture. "Follow me." And so I followed her silently for a while as we headed toward the forest on the outskirts of the sanctuary. I wondered what she expected from me. I rifled through my brain and was reminded how I was both disinterested and unskilled when it came to making small talk. What constituted small talk for her anyways if she was really three millennia old? Soon enough, we were in the thick of the forest. Surrounded by the green canopy, the crunch of dead leaves echoed from beneath my sandal steps.

"Is your name really Diana?" I asked. "Simon said that you were four millennia old, but the name Diana is the Roman equivalent of the goddess Artemis from Greek mythology, and those were a bit more recent in history . . ."

Diana sighed. "My native language is difficult to translate into English, so Diana was a close enough name. I came from a band of hunter-gatherers, and I loved to shoot with bows ever since I was a toddler, so when I heard of the stories of Artemis and Diana, I decided to adopt the name. It's less stupid than what you let yourself be called, right, Abyss?"

I couldn't remember either my first or last name and shrugged. "Maybe I can go by John Smith . . . Abyss John Smith." Diana didn't seem to find the joke funny, and I continued. "So does being immortal mean that you have to remain a hunter-gatherer?" I asked. "Did you just give up on forming any human connections due to outliving everyone?"

"Who knows?" Diana asked. "I heard the Witch that you contracted with has immense power, so perhaps she might be able to restore me to a normal life. But I've gotten used to being disappointed over the years." The forest was opening to reveal large, grassy plains of orange and yellow blades. In the distance, I could see many wild animals grazing, and I couldn't see a highway or a city over the horizon. "As for your first question, I've tried many times to adapt to the so-called luxuries of modernity, but at my heart, I've always thought nature produced the greatest beauty and experiences. There was a Witch who also believed strongly in doing so, and so she created hidden natural landscapes like these, although even her power is no match for humanity's tendencies to ravage entire ecosystems."

"Well, you can't blame me for being used to living in a house or a city," I said. "Can't we do our training there? At least tell me that we can check into a hotel and stuff and that you have identities prepared. I'm willing to be Abyss John Smith or whatever stupid name you want me to take. Speaking of which, you've used last names before, right? It might not be the most common name, but . . ."

Diana was trying hard not to slap me, it seemed. "Sobekhotep."

"So be what?"

"Diana Sobekhotep, if you insist on two names making a full name." The last name she attached didn't seem to be either Greek or Roman, but on the other hand, it didn't seem like she was just stringing together syllables. "And no, we aren't checking into a hotel. It's still summer, so you won't freeze out here, and I can show you how to make good shelter by working leaves and dead branches."

"If that's essential for my quest," I muttered. "So when do we begin training? Sonny taught me the basics of boxing, but I guess it couldn't help for me to learn some archery as well. And I don't mean to pry, but how did you become immortal anyways? What will happen if you don't properly train me?"

"It's nothing as straightforward as being incentivized by a punishment," Diana said. "Just as human beings can't control unconscious movements like beating their heart, I can't opt out of training heroes. And I'm not training you in any particular field of combat, even if you think being a hero is similar to being a government-funded military class. I'm going to teach you how to survive and stick around until you manage to control your powers, and then I'll be done with my duty. Are you hungry?" Diana asked.

"I got a small bite after all the chaos that happened this morning, so no . . . " I started.

"But you will be hungry in three or four hours," Diana said. "I'm not going to hunt down animals just for a spoiled prince." Again, she was using that term, and I decided to fire back.

"Have you even really tried the modern world before dismissing us as spoiled?" I asked. "Thanks to research and development, we've prevented famine, eradicated plagues with vaccines, increased productivity with electricity, and, well, we know . . . we broadened our understanding of the universe through science. Sure, we might not be the best at surviving in a savannah or tundra or desert, and there might be some negative environmental impacts, but you don't have to be so stubborn with your hunter-gatherer pride . . ."

"But in the end, with all of that progress, you've only created new ways to delude yourselves," Diana said. "Creating video games instead of playing outside, developing foods so unhealthy that the majority of your population suffers from obesity, and overworking yourselves in little cubicles all for getting more green wads of cash or raising the number in a computerized checking account. While nomadic tribes herd their animals with grace and diligence, you just cram all of nature's creations into little pens and sheds and factories, pump them full of drugs, and thoughtlessly consume meat."

I couldn't really reply to Diana regarding that observation. Humans had made life better for humans, but produced genocides and ecological devastation when it came to the fauna and flora of the earth. "All right, so it's still early in the afternoon," I observed. "And in a grassy field, I can't really set up traps, so you basically want me to chase something down until it collapses from heat exhaustion. That's called persistence hunting, right?"

"I'll go easy on you and give you a spear and help with creating fire, too," Diana said. "For once, I want one of these modern humans to understand what it means to truly earn meat in his belly. Many times, hunts fail, but you won't starve in a day. I'll direct you to some water and edible roots if that happens, and we can try again tomorrow."

Diana headed over to a long, fallen tree branch from the forest area and made quick work with her stone knives. She created a reasonably straight spear by tying a sharp stone to one of its ends. I wasn't exactly sure where she got all of her thin rope, and I realized that I had a lot to learn from this immortal hunter-gatherer.

"Thanks," I said as I took the spear and practiced some awkward throws.

"Here's a knife as well to make the finishing cut," Diana said as she handed me one of her stone knives. "Watch out for predator tracks, and don't try anything stupid just because you managed to draw out the diamond blade earlier."

"Mountain lions and bears, got it," I mumbled. This secret reserve of nature seemed to contain creatures like impalas grazing on the plains, which should be native to Africa. I wondered if lions and hyenas were enough for this new quest that Diana was sending me on, or if I would have to deal with more odd monsters.

Being able to sneak up and get a solid hit in through stealth hunting was far preferable to the exhaustion of persistence hunting, and so that would be my initial strategy. But unfortunately, I had no experience when it came to sneaking up quietly, and the animals grazing the fields were neither sick nor injured enough to make getting a cheap shot easy.

"This'll have to do," I muttered to myself as I threw the spear as far as I could. It was off-target by a good meter or so as the impala that I'd aimed for bolted. I quickly jogged forward and picked up my spear to chase after the impala.

Now, I really wished that I had Simon's teleportation ability. Perhaps even Sonny's temporary status boost would be enough to chase down one of these impalas, and maybe Justin could do something with his incantations. I quickly realized how much slower two legs were compared to four and why nature had developed very few bipeds that lacked flight.

In the tall grass, the impala quickly became a speck of brown fur in the distance and joined a new small band of other impalas. I tried to keep my eye on my target as much as possible, but I knew that luck wasn't on my side. I would most likely pick the wrong impala to continue chasing after, and they would blend into the herd and continuously scatter so that each of them would have a fair time to rest.

So then it would go back to more training my spear throw than anything else. I didn't know which impala was my original target, but I went for the one that seemed to fear me the least. Another spear throw proved a meter off-target, and as I started to chase after the animal, I felt my pains and aches from earlier in the day begin to act up. I shook my head and closed my eyes. I would try to invoke a sort of sixth sense and hoped that the diamond blade would erupt from the ground yet again and do the work for me. But all I heard was the stillness of the air as I felt beads of sweat trickle down my head, and I sighed as I opened my eyes. I could only trek after the nearest herd of impala.

Primal sense began to creep into my mind. It was a thought, but it lacked any rudimentary language to describe it, as if my brain had regressed to that of a chimp. But even then, it was enough of a hint for me. I was feeling what one of the animals was feeling, at first relaxed that I was moving in the wrong direction, and then anxious that this odd biped exploring the plains was somehow able to smell fear despite having such a small nose. I didn't lock onto the animal's thoughts that I was reading, but I could deduct its general location, and I broke into a light jog, my spear ready in my hands.

This time, I didn't chuck the spear. Rather, it was my odd sixth sense that I would use to chase after and exhaust the animal before killing it. The abstract thought hit my brain before it developed into language. *Slow, my predator is slow. But he doesn't stop.* Again, as I gave chase, the impala turned into a brown speck of fur and found yet another herd. I felt the train of thought and emotion break off, as if my sixth sense only worked in a certain range. But my only hope was to keep jogging and keep my prey hopelessly running, so I let sweat drench my face and chest as my ankles whined and my mind grew dizzy.

When I reached the herd of impala and continued my chase, I struggled to reestablish a connection with my prey. I'd scared off at least four other impala and felt nothing. Now I really wondered how the tribal ancestors had hunted without a sixth sense. The fifth impala I chased after gave me the mental link, however, and my mind grew even dizzier. My vision blurred as the sweat on my body turned into small bursts of dancing flames, and now I realized I was feeling what the impala was feeling. Most animals weren't built for endurance. These creatures were adept at outrunning lions and even cheetahs, but the human hunter was something far too bizarre.

Despite my blurry vision, I continued to give chase. I was sure that at least an hour had passed as I repeated this process. The mental connection broke apart a few times whenever the impala managed to escape into the distance. But each time I found it in the herd, its fears and exhaustion became more pronounced, easier to sense, and more impactful on my own brain as the bearer of this sixth sense.

"Sorry, pal," I muttered softly as I continued the chase. The impala was still running faster than me but slowed down from its initial speed. It wasn't just about finding dinner this evening — I also wanted to prove myself to Diana and further develop my mysterious power.

Strange, the impala's thoughts now read. *Slow and strange.* And then jolts of fear and adrenaline were the creature's last remaining hopes, but it was already overheated. It felt like I was leaping between the impala's sensory experience and my own so that I would constantly switch from baking in the summer heat with a coat full of fur to feeling the cool relief of a sweat-stained shirt and face.

Can't go on, the impala thought to itself as it finally slowed down to a human jogging pace. *Will die . . .*

I only had a little more work to do, and I wasn't sure if the remainder of the chase took fifteen minutes or another hour. But finally, the impala collapsed on a barren section of the grasslands, and I gave a silent cheer to myself.

"Does it really have to end this way, though?" I asked as I raised my spear. The impala looked at me. Its vision was probably blurred from exhaustion. He must have been confused that I lacked mighty fangs and claws or even envious of my ability to sweat and cool down. Even if the creature wasn't as cute as a kitten or a puppy, even if it couldn't read or write or speak, I knew it was cursing its fate and questioning the insanity of the world. I then shook my head.

Learning about the food chain was elementary school material, and learning that humans were brutal in factory farming wasn't much farther ahead. This impala had a better life than the vast majority of animals bred for meat, and I had eaten meat and eggs without any serious attempts to go vegan. I wouldn't let some other predator come and take the prey that I'd labored for hours chasing. I walked closer and closer to make sure that I wouldn't miss my spear throw. I probably couldn't hit the neck, so I just aimed for the center of the creature's mass as I threw the projectile.

The impala didn't thrash as the spear sunk through its fur and deep into its flesh. But it was still alive, and it might take hours to bleed out. I took the stone knife that Diana had given me and crept forward, watching the impala throw out a pathetic kick that even a first-grader could dodge. Now I was up to the creature's neck, and worst of all, the mental connection that I'd made with my magic hadn't quite disappeared. I felt the fear and bewilderment, the confusion of losing to a creature that had to create and equip himself with weapons before hunting but had ended up being far more effective than the beasts on all fours. I forced myself to empty my mind as I sunk the knife deep into the impala's neck.

Like a machine, I dragged the knife across the thick of the creature's neck and watched a large stream of blood pour out like a waterfall, which signaled that I'd finished my task. But my concentration snapped there, and I felt what the impala felt. It was pure shock and horror at impending death, desperately wishing for some afterlife, a mix between sorrow and lust for revenge. My head grew woozy from the fragments of the impala thoughts constantly bombarding my normal attempts at reason and language, and I felt that I'd gone above and beyond Diana's goal of connecting to nature. As the impala's thoughts grew more scattered and incomplete from its massive blood loss, my brain was unable to keep up with the shadows of death, and I fell into unconsciousness.

"Wake up. Wake up, Abyss."

I had the most wonderful dream that I'd been going on an adventure to restore some mysterious diamond blade, and . . .

"Abyss!" Since when was that my nickname? I'd probably stayed up too late at night reading weird horror stories. I even dreamt that I was transferring thoughts with an impala of all creatures as I hunted it down on the hot grasslands . . .

"Abyss!"

Lights and shadows finally made their way into my vision, and as I saw the figure of the brown-skinned girl with cheetah lines on her cheeks come into vision, I instinctively darted away in fear, crawling on all fours. What was I doing? One of these furless bipeds had just hunted me down, even though I consistently outran him.

Why do my legs feel so weird, and why is my vision so narrow?

I collapsed onto my side as I attempted to further run like an impala, and as air filled my lungs, I finally snapped into the wretched human form. I was a lucky member of the only species of great ape that had smoothly transitioned to bipedalism, the ones that ended up dominating the globe even before they made radical leaps in technology.

"*Aagrhrhr* . . . " I tried to relearn how to form my vocal chords and find language. "Dia . . . Diana?" I asked. It was sunset now, which meant that I'd at least slept for a couple of hours from my epic hunt in the hot afternoon.

"I don't know how you did it, but you got him, all right," Diana said. "But were you that tired that you fell asleep right after you killed him?"

"I . . . It must be my power," I tried to explain. "At first, I didn't know what it was. It manifested as an ability to pseudo-mind read, and I was able to block swords and punches alike for thirty seconds or so when I was at the sanctuary." Diana didn't seem familiar with such a power. "Because of my ability, I was able to continue tracking down the original impala that I'd targeted when it kept running away and disappearing into the herd. And when I slit the creature's throat, its fear and thoughts transferred over to me and ended up being so overwhelming that I died and thought that I was an impala when I woke up."

Diana chuckled. "That's one heck of a magical power to grant. But I would expect no less of the legendary Witch, who cannot be named."

I sighed. "Even if we can't meet up, I wish she would just deliver me an instruction manual or something," I said. I noticed that Diana was already beginning to set up shelter now and was adept at gathering medium-sized branches and leaves to create a small hut. Carving small holes in the tough dirt was enough for her to balance the initial supporting beams, which she began to further reinforce with her thin ropes.

"I wanted to teach you how to gut and skin the carcass, but since you were passed out for so long, we can probably focus on building shelter and making fire."

"Sounds like fun," I said as I got up to my feet and quickly realized that I was still tired from the day's activities. "Well, are you still disappointed in me?" I asked. "My ability might have given me an unfair advantage, but I can hunt like any of the men and boys in your tribe, right?"

"Just get to gathering branches." Diana gestured to the hut that she was building. "You won't be sharing this with me, so whatever you can collect by the end of the night will be what you sleep in."

It would probably be dark in less than an hour. I still didn't like my power, but I wanted to keep my chin up. This was only the beginning, and it was perhaps more than most heroes from fantasy stories got as they made their endless march on their quests. I gathered the best assortment of fallen branches and twigs that I could, but as I brought them back to Diana's settlement and started building my hut, I realized that it would be pathetic for creating cover. I was truly glad that it was summer, for if I'd been taken here in winter, I would likely freeze to death.

"Any suggestions?" I asked as I turned to Diana.

"You just need more experience," she said, decidedly. She now gestured to her gathering of dry leaves and grass. "Give the bow and spindle a try. I'm sure that you can handle it, right?"

My successful hunt for the impala would be my only victory today, it appeared. Diana let me struggle with the bow and spindle for well over an hour. She let me create hot bundles of smoke and black charred wood, but I had no luck starting the spark that would allow me to cook my hard-earned meal.

"My hands are burning with blisters," I griped, having failed to achieve visible smoke. Finally after the sky went dark, she gave it a try. Her speed and dexterity with her fingers were impressive, and although she began with a couple of failed ashes, she was able to produce an ember in less than ten minutes, and as she fed the spark dry leaves, grass, and oxygen, a blaze of orange-yellow lit up in the dark night.

"Thank you," I said as I turned over to the impala carcass. "I don't suppose you could teach me how to cook either?" My stomach was growling, but I still doubted that I could eat the entire impala.

"I can't create meals like your spoiled generation can," Diana admitted. "But I can smoke, salt, and spice up meats in order to preserve them as jerky. I'm not letting any of this meat go to waste. I honestly didn't expect you to come back with anything more than a stupid rabbit to catch off-guard or maybe some eggs from a bird's nest." With a few twigs, the fire began to grow big enough to become a cooking fire and strong enough to sustain on larger branches.

"I could use some of the pelt for the winter as well," I said. "Assuming that we're going to be in the wild for that long." Diana was content to make shish-kabobs with the breast meat, and I simply held the impala's ankle out to roast over the bare flames. I wasn't sure when the meat would be perfectly tender, but it was probably better to be a little burnt than risk consuming undercooked flesh. Diana then fell into silence for a while, uninterested in any small talk this spoiled generation could make, and I smiled a little.

Even if Diana was no princess, this wasn't bad for my first date, was it? She probably didn't consider it such, but I had hardly talked to girls at all before this. Our hunter-gatherer ancestors had probably lived this way for thousands of years, and perhaps Diana was correct that modernity made humans too shallow and materialistic. I looked up at the starry night, which was a foreign sight to me given the light pollution from houses and cities, and was again reminded of another problem.

"Are you truly immortal?" I asked Diana. "What will you do when the sun consumes Earth in a billion years, or at least makes it too hot for any life to survive on it? The best thing we can do is attempt to terraform planets close to us." Diana allowed me to continue, and so I went on. "Of course it's pretty far-fetched even if we can reach light-speed, as Alpha Centauri is around four light-years from us. But still, assuming you survive that with your magic, and the sun simply becomes a supernova rather than a black hole . . . you'd just be stranded on a dead planet waiting for the aliens."

"If you manage to develop such inter-stellar technologies one day, I might hitch a ride," Diana said. "But regarding your initial point, I'm not truly immortal. I don't age, but I can die of disease or fatal injury, and it's happened at least a dozen times. When that happens, though, the next human or two that wanders too close to my burial place, perhaps deemed by fate or magic, eventually becomes the flesh and blood I need to re-spawn. So if the human race goes extinct, I'll probably lose my ability to re-spawn."

"That's pretty . . . dark," I muttered. I turned over my impala ankle and felt that it was getting a little burnt. Diana's shish-kabob was done already as she began popping the chunks of meat into her mouth. She didn't seem too worried about dying or enthusiastic about living—if this was a book or a video game, I wondered if I would just meet the true love interest later. But romance or no romance, it was good that I had her after I'd gotten rejected at the Western Sanctuary, although I wished Sonny could have come along on my quest.

As I bit into the impala leg, I realized that it was indeed slightly burnt, but my hungry stomach certainly didn't care for that fact. "So what's the plan for tomorrow, fake-goddess?"

Diana shrugged. "Aside from helping you with basic survival skills, the quest you have is unique," she admitted. "Since you were the one that pulled out the diamond blade, you'll lead us in the direction we need to go to restore it." I continued to chomp down on the impala leg until I was full, and I handed the rest of the meat to Diana.

"Now I wish we had a refrigerator," I said. "It's no burger and fries, but honestly wasn't bad." I felt a bit of a food coma come over me as I headed into my poorly constructed hut. I wondered if I would have another dream of being an impala and hoped that I'd find something useful regarding my power and the Witch I contracted with. As I faded into unconsciousness, my vision escaped from my body, and I started to see the world rewind.

Described precisely, it was as if I was a cameraman following Diana, and everything was set to quickly rewind. Centuries passed within a few seconds, and everything spun back for thousands of nights and days until I was at the beginning of the girl's lifespan, when she was a mere mortal.

"Oh, wow, you're here already." Another person had joined in to observe this flashback — it was Diana, but with a warmer smile and friendlier voice, as if she hadn't been desensitized by the passing of thousands of years.

"Already?" I asked. "Was I supposed to do more work in order to meet this hidden side of you?"

"Who knows?" Diana asked. "I oftentimes think that I'm the real me, while the Diana you meet outside of your dreams claims I'm a fake version, as well." When we started seeing Diana's lifespan, I'd expected time to flow normally, but instead, it felt like I was watching a poorly directed documentary that often skipped long segments and events. This was probably the nature of human memory, and just like the impala, I'd been able to somehow connect to Diana's train of thought.

"Hunter-gatherers," I observed. "Sounds like a fun existence, huh?" Upon watching Diana's memories, it did feel like the people in her tribe were much more genuine than most adults I remembered meeting, probably simply due to having a larger amount of free time. The kids didn't seem particularly unhappy with life, and even though there were always at least a couple of child mortalities each year from disease or accidents, they didn't dwell on the grief. The most common games I saw them play were tag, hide and seek, and climbing trees, and the adults didn't stop brawls and wrestling matches unless they got really dangerous. It was a world without academic pressure, fashion trends, or worrying about who made the school sports teams.

"I was around thirteen when the incident happened," Diana explained to me. "While many girls at that age were wed off, I was stubborn about getting married and stood up to the tribal elder. Since I was good at archery and helped on hunts, they let me for a while, but . . . " Diana's voice trailed off. "We were in the way of a greater power, an empire."

The train of memories I observed once again continued to scatter as a large army of hundreds of soldiers came to invade Diana's small tribe of around thirty. It appeared that the empire's army and the hunter-gatherers could hardly understand each other, as best as they tried to convey themselves through body language. I couldn't understand either language, and when violence eventually broke out, there was no magic miracle, no diamond blade to save Diana's tribe. The men who didn't surrender were slaughtered with the exception of one tall, muscular man who'd managed to kill three of the empire's soldiers with only two knives in his hands before being captured. Perhaps he would either be tortured with a later death or conscripted into the army. When Diana surrendered to the empire's troops, they'd curiously inspected her, and the tones of their voice changed from aggression to intrigue.

"I think most of my tribe became slaves, forced to work to death as they built pyramids or walls," the present Diana commentated as she stood at my side. "I knew that I probably should be considered lucky, as they thought that my pretty face was too much to waste." Still, I saw her bicker against the soldiers in response as she attempted to whack at them with her bow. The soldiers chuckled at the futile attempt and easily wrestled and bound her wrists with rope.

"Rha ka Pharaoh," I heard one of the soldiers say. The train of memories continued to skip about until I found Diana serving in a palace dressed in much fancier clothing. She was apparently now fluently speaking the language of her new empire. The black cheetah lines on her cheeks were wiped away to suit her new role. Suddenly, a magical spell washed over me, and I could understand every language being spoken.

"This is where the memories become clearer," Diana said. "In addition to the trauma, I was also forced to forget everything about my previous life in order to serve the emperor. Heh." Her voice sounded surprisingly faint and somber upon going through this section of her memory. "I'm sure many girls, both peasants and hunter-gatherers would trade what they had for the life that I got." Diana appeared to be one of the many concubines in the emperor's harem — or rather, the Pharaoh, given that she'd been taken to a kingdom in ancient Egypt. "I wore many pretty dresses and tasted many delicacies that I would otherwise never experience if I had remained a hunter-gatherer. But . . . concubines weren't allowed to go out and hunt and practice archery. That was one thing."

The train of memories shifted over to one of the moments where Diana had a private conversation with the Pharaoh himself. "Please let my tribe, my friends, and family go free," she was begging the Pharaoh. He wasn't as fat and spoiled as I had anticipated, and many muscles adorned his tall frame underneath the jewelry and robes that adorned his shoulders. His caramel skin and full beard made him almost look like a mythical demigod, even when compared to Simon's handsome figure.

"I consulted the prophets, and they have said that it was destined by Ra himself that your little tribe will only produce two people worthy of my empire," the Pharaoh said. "The rest are only good for building the pyramids. It's been quite a few months now, and yet you still haven't quite learned your place amongst the other concubines, have you?" I could see the fear in young Diana's eyes, as if she'd been brainwashed just enough to believe in the divinity of the man she was serving under. If I could step into this flashback, I would run up and punch the Pharaoh.

"Your Highness," Diana continued. "The food, clothing, and luxuries of your palace are excellent, but it's still very unfair to force the majority of your population to work as peasants, as slaves, and soldiers. Even if I managed to be lucky, I can't stop thinking that life would be better in a tribe for humans overall . . ."

"Foolish girl you are," the Pharaoh interrupted. "You can only see the shortcomings of the present day and fail to imagine the future. Did your tribe ever chart the motion of the stars or build wonders like the pyramids you see outside the window? I don't know how many years it will take, but mankind will make progress. One day, we'll see what the stars are made of and witness the beginning of creation. We'll learn about the secrets of the human body and cure outbreaks of disease, and every young girl will reap the benefits of invention and progress and be able to be just as beautiful as you are, *Drsyna*." It was a slightly different name that the Pharaoh had given her, impossible for an English speaker to pronounce.

"And perhaps the common man will live even more comfortably than I will as a Pharaoh, and we'll go beyond narrating the Epic of Gilgamesh to simulate a world where everyone can be a hero." The Pharaoh turned to Diana and saw the doubt in her eyes. "Every king or emperor thinks alike, but I have gone above and beyond and made contracts with the Witches of this world. The world will remember how far I've spurred humanity with my civilizations and forget about your little backwater tribe. They will remember the Pharaoh Sobekhotep!"

That was when the memory began to blur, and light flooded in from the edges of the disordered string of thoughts.

I woke up in a daze and felt leaves and twigs prick at my back. I was sore from sleeping on my pathetic attempts to construct a proper bed, and as I crawled out of my shoddy hut, Diana eyed me with an annoyed look on her face.

"I know that you went snooping around last night," she said.

"I don't control what my dreams are," I began to protest. "I mean . . . I think I understand you a bit more now."

"Hah," Diana said as she checked her equipment and continued her project from last night. She was twisting together grass, intestines, and anything suitable to make more string and rope for later use and making sure to sharpen a few spare arrowheads. "What do you understand? You're cute now, but in a few years, and if you manage to awaken and abuse the power that you received from the Witch, then you'll end up like every Pharaoh and emperor in history. You'll have your own palace, your own harem, and your own personal servants to boss around and probably get caught up in a dumb war due to your ego."

I shrugged and tried to quickly fire back with what I knew about the world. "Well, it's a fancier way of what animals do already. There's always been an alpha in wolf packs or gorilla communities if we want to discuss closer relatives. For now . . . I just want to do what I can to save lives and improve the life quality of those that I can't save. That's why I was chosen to be a hero, right?"

"Well, some heroes have contributed to such goals," Diana admitted. "But given that you pulled out the diamond blade, it seems like the God of Fire expects chaos out of your life more than anything else. Well, chaos means more adventure, and I guess that's part of what people dream of in a hero story, isn't it?"

"So then, will you teach me how to build a proper hut and

bed now? Or maybe I could try my hands at archery myself. If you want me to chase down another impala, I won't complain either, although I'm still a bit sore from yesterday's hunt."

"I will follow you and see where your quest leads," Diana decided. "Your magical power has awakened, both with the impala and with snooping into my memories, so it should give you a hint on where to go next. I'll help locate and gather water, and you can have the rest of the impala jerky that I preserved for you."

Diana was rather quiet as I led the way through the seemingly endless grasslands. In all honesty, it was surprisingly boring compared to how action-packed many adventure stories had become in the modern era. But Diana was probably used to boredom given how long she'd lived, and if I complained, it would probably just reinforce the notion that I was spoiled.

"Do you know what we need?" I suddenly asked. "We need a ship, random sea monsters, and also a good cook that only uses his feet when fighting so his hands are clean." Diana didn't seem amused by the suggestion. "I know that human beings have abused and manipulated nature's bounty," I remembered the memories from the dream last night. "But can't you admit that we've made some progress? Only in the last few centuries has hand washing and soap become commonplace, and thanks to that, we've reduced child mortality."

Diana shrugged. "Only to force unhealthy food down children's throats and cram them into buildings where they're hunched over on endless worksheets," she decided.

"Have you even tried sports?" I wondered. "Basketball can be fun, and if we lack proper equipment, soccer is always possible with the availability of rubber balls. Wall-ball was also a thing in elementary school . . . " I caught myself, realizing how awkward I was. In this sense, it was lucky that Diana was my first female friend, given that she wouldn't judge me for being *uncool*.

"If the modern world was so fun, why have you developed so many drugs?" Diana asked. "Alcohol, tobacco, marijuana, heroin, the list goes on and on, with new addicts to treat every year." It appeared that this conversation really was getting nowhere. I scanned the horizon and suddenly felt my heartbeat thump.

"Something's happening over there!" I gestured. The endless grasslands didn't seem to be so endless after all, for as Diana and I broke into a jog, it was clear that a small village was in the distance as white-purple rifts appeared in the sky. As we made our way closer, it was as if the Pharaoh's army that I'd seen in my dreams had suddenly been resurrected. Men were clad in ancient armor and equipped with spears and swords alike.

"It can't be . . . " Diana began as she turned to me with an angry expression. "All because you pulled out the diamond blade and let the God of Fire work his chaos!"

"We've got to stop them!" I said as I led the way. The resurrected soldiers attacked the villagers indiscriminately and ruthlessly chucked spears at whatever unlucky victim was in range. Diana was hesitant as I entered the city, and I nervously grabbed the stone knife that she lent me. I wanted the diamond blade to rise from the ground yet again and carry me through battle, but I remembered that the entire purpose of my quest was to avoid using the diamond blade until I'd sealed the God of Fire. "Support me with arrow fire!" I said to Diana.

The villagers that had been speared didn't bleed to death, but perhaps began to morph into something more gruesome. Their skin and organs began to turn inside out as if hundreds of new tumors were spreading across their bodies, and the resulting flesh was half-liquid, which seeped toward the rifts in space-time that were occurring. One tall man in light armor was barking commands at the rest of the soldiers. It seemed he was requesting that a few survivors be left alive for whatever reason.

Without the diamond blade to guide me, my only chance of victory was confronting the commander directly. "Hey!" I yelled as I ran toward him, waving my arms. "Hey! Tell your men to knock it off!" Diana was trailing behind me with her bow in hand, and she apparently agreed that this was the optimal strategy.

The tall commander looked at me with his well-trimmed beard and laughed.

"*Gryashke,*" Diana began in her native tribal language. "*Anaskprovormaloprus, sinekar . . .* " Now I wished that there was a translator around as she started to exchange words with the commander. She didn't seem entirely hostile to the army's commander, who only smiled and dismissed her concerns. I probably let around a minute of their dialogue pass before butting in.

"Could you two please speak in English?" I yelled, and the army commander chuckled once more. Maybe this was the moment where I would discover my true enemy, just like in a classic video game where he would easily overpower me. I didn't care how pathetic I looked at the time, and I was prepared to be beaten worse than I had been when I fought against Simon.

"Where are my manners?" the commander asked. "You can call me Grigory. That would be an easy name to pronounce for your generation, right? And you need not act so hostile toward me, young one. We're on the same side, after all, chosen by the God of Fire for the same reasons."

"Same side?" I asked. My patience grew thin. The commander barked orders to his men, and for a while, they stopped spearing the villagers and transforming them into fleshy liquid.

"You wanted to be a hero, and heroes do what most men cannot," Grigory started, turning back toward Diana. "You have seen modern man use, abuse, and spoil himself by perverting nature, have you not? The weak and sickly, the stupid and lazy survive and reproduce, abandoning the very qualities that enabled our dominance during evolution. To put it in simple terms, we're here to purge mankind of its weaker elements and let its remainders grow and prosper."

I shook my head upon hearing such an explanation. "From twentieth-century eugenicists to unoriginal villains of TV shows, that's a really lame way to justify evil," I said. I wondered if there was any way to negotiate with Grigory, but if bargaining failed, I was ready to jump into combat.

"You're just brainwashed," Diana began. Stubborn anger and worry both showed on her face. "You were the other one from our village that Sobekhotep decided to spare, weren't you? I thought you would fight to the bitter end, but you crumbled to one of his powerful magical spells, didn't you?"

"I merely learned the truth when I stepped outside of our little hunter-gatherer tribe," Grigory declared. "My talents, the life that nature gave me, would waste away if I stayed in my original tribe. From an early age, victory came too easy for me in boxing and wrestling, and I was the only man who could consistently have successful hunts, as well. Although you were a close second. When the Pharaoh put me into the Coliseum to determine if I was fit for his army, I finally met the competition I needed to become stronger." Grigory then turned back to me. "Hasn't your generation discovered the truth now that science has progressed so far? You discovered that at the end of life, there will be no god to complete your purpose and redeem your poor souls. The reason that we're speaking language instead of barking and screeching is because evolution had put pressure on our ancestors' shoulders to communicate. When humanity made life too comfortable for itself, the best future has now come to rely on machinery for simulation and stimulation."

"But evolution has no end goal because there's an endless amount of varying environments," I said. I remembered the clerics and priests who had attacked the Western Sanctuary, and I wasn't keen on joining them either. "Even if evil and weakness exist in our population, I don't quite think it can be weeded out by the process of randomly killing people." Grigory looked rather disappointed in me as he gestured to his troops.

"Keep Diana out of this," Grigory commanded as he raised his arms in a fighting position. I slowly shadowed his movements as we began to circle around. I was nervously sweating and hoped that my sixth sense would at least be enough to point me in the right direction, just like it had done with the gazelle.

"I was chosen by this legendary Witch because I saved a girl from a truck," I started. "And the Western Sanctuary told me that Witches and their heroes aimed to save humanity . . ."

"Only by letting some of the population rightfully fail and die will humanity be saved," Grigory decided as he threw the first punch. I knew that at this level, he was just playing with me, and his punches were easy to block and dodge. But he was no slouch on defense. He scoffed as he blocked every punch I threw. I wasn't able to read his thoughts or movements like I had with the gazelle. Or rather, I was getting a faint mental image, but everything was moving too fluidly, as if I was trying to measure water that was continuously swirling around in a glass beaker.

A simple feint was enough to throw me off-guard, and a hard left fist slammed into my left cheek. I collapsed onto the ground, and unlike the other heroes at the Western Sanctuary, Grigory wasn't content with letting me back up. "The legendary Witch chose you for a reason," Grigory grumbled as he started kicking me wherever his foot would land. I was getting bruises on my chest, abdomen, and my groin, and when Grigory was finished kicking my front, he grabbed me by the collar and looked me eye to eye.

"*Gryash!*" Diana started to protest, and I could hear her struggle against Grigory's underlings. My vision was blurry from all the pain, but I knew that this was my best opportunity to inflict serious damage. I tried to throw the best head-butt I could, aiming for Grigory's nose, and darkness and stars filled my vision as Grigory let go of me, and I slumped onto the ground once more.

"Ahahaha!" Grigory was laughing of all things and had prepared for my desperate gambit. Instead of hitting the soft cartilage of his nose, my skull had simply crashed against his, and I felt how years of training must have toughened his bones. I forced myself to my feet and still wobbled as I tried to search for Diana. If I couldn't even scar Grigory, the best I could do was try to save as many other lives as possible, perhaps create another distraction . . .

Thud. Grigory was ready to box yet again, and a fist collided with my stomach. My legs shook and shivered, but I remained on my feet, insistent on dying like a hero. A flock of birds, large enough to be geese were passing overhead, and I heard their squawks and caws ring about my ear. *Slam.*

"Let's bet on how many punches this hero can withstand!" Some of Grigory's men spoke up. "Five more? Six more? Seven?"

I must have sustained enough internal damage to begin hallucinating—as Grigory continuously pummeled me with punches, shadows of creatures from the Cretaceous, Jurassic, and Triassic period began to roam across the ground. An allosaurus pack attempted to hunt down a stegosaurus while our mammalian ancestors scurried about in holes and bushes.

Sixty-five million years passed, and humans did their best to live in peace and prosperity, but apparently, Grigory believed that heroes should spur their species to evolve even further.

The shadows of the long-extinct species began to flow through the ground and up to me, as if they had finally found a proper vessel for reincarnation. Even if I couldn't shape-shift at will, some part of me had to change and perhaps become monstrous if I was to survive this fight against Grigory . . .

"Eight punches!" One of the men exclaimed. "And the boy's still standing! If he'd been born in our generation, perhaps he would have become a fine warrior . . ."

"Shut up . . . " I muttered as I gritted my teeth. Grigory shot a punch toward my head to finish things off, as his knuckles were definitely harder than my skull. But the shadows I'd gathered from the age of the dinosaurs were pulsing all through my bloodstream, and my right arm shivered, almost exploded as the muscles began to harden and reform. In a ruthless fury, I took the blow full-force, and I aimed to crush Grigory's throat. And for the first time in this grueling battle, I saw surprise and fear in his eyes as he got his left arm up just in time.

My right hand clamped on Grigory's left forearm, digging into the soft flesh as my nails had transformed into talons. Or rather, my entire right arm had mutated into something foreign—part of it was hardened brown scales covered with what appeared to be diamond plating. However, it was just my right arm that had been able to transform, and the pain in my shoulder prevented me from properly moving it around my socket. "You beat me up and break some ribs, I take out one of your arms," I decided.

Grigory laughed again, though, this time a little nervously. "So the Witch chose the right person to contract with after all." Grigory was flexing as hard as he could, but my new talons were digging through his muscles and would soon snap bone.

"Commander!" many of Grigory's underlings shouted in dismay, but Grigory waved them off with his free hand.

"He's a worthy hero after all, channeling the rage, anguish, and ambition of the extinct," Grigory decided. "We've collected enough flesh-matter in this area. And on top of that, we've activated the key to our Pharaoh's resurrection. I like you, boy. What was your name again?"

"Abyss," I grumbled, still unable to remember my actual name. I could hear the ligaments in my right arm cracking, and was frustrated that I would have to settle for taking one of Grigory's arms. "And I'll never work for your Pharaoh, as I'll fight for Diana's sake, as well as the world's!" Grigory chuckled as his arm popped off, purple gas and black steam hissing from his lost limb instead of a trail of blood. Black oil spiraled through my mutated arm as I stumbled back, sore and battered.

"Abyss, what a name for a boy! Perhaps he'll be the first hero that doesn't fail you, huh?" Grigory turned to Diana as he gestured his men toward the rift in space-time. "But now that our Pharaoh is returning, you're free to serve him anytime you choose. I'm sure you'll come to your senses eventually, old friend." With that, Grigory was the last one to jump into the portal, and reality began to mostly normalize.

"Next time I'll . . . " I cursed under my breath as I felt the hairs on my right arm begin to curl and pop, which revealed the sheer amount of pressure that I'd put on them through the transformation. The bruises that had formed all over my body were also beginning to quake and pull at my sanity. I sunk to my knees as I heard Diana rush to my side and began to fade into unconsciousness.

CHAPTER THREE

I wasn't greeted with pleasant dreams of the gentle Diana, but was shaken awake by the stubborn cheetah-cheeked hunter.

"You were out for a couple of hours," she said as I began to stir. I wish that she'd brought me back to the hospital bed at the Western Sanctuary instead of some clearing in this large forest. *I really could use one of Ruth's special lime juice to heal my bruises and relieve my exhaustion. Heck, I would settle for an actual hospital.* But when I looked around and proceeded to examine my right arm, I quickly discovered why Diana had decided against that idea.

"So, uh . . . " I started as I attempted to form a fist with my right arm. I would probably have difficulty grabbing things until it healed, and what was worse was that it appeared to be infected by large, black warts, and purple veins bulged through attempting to fight the foreign infection. It looked less like the arm of a demon or dragon's, and more like every shape and size of tumor had tried to cram themselves into my muscle and cartilage. Right now, I would perhaps fit more into a horror movie rather than be the subject of a superhero comic book. "You ever see this before?"

"No. I recognize neither the sudden mutation you pulled off nor the aftermath with what's going on with your arm," Diana observed. "I considered amputating it but realized that you might be a rare hero who was gifted more than one power, since you contracted with the legendary Witch, after all." My nose suddenly felt sharper, but I could only smell one

56

foreign trail.

"Smells like . . . a giant gas leak at the gas station," I said. "And it's coming from that direction." I pointed with my mutated arm. "Before my arm mutated, I saw the ancient remnants of dinosaurs and stuff dissolve into shadow and feed me," I tried to recall my memories. "And when I originally made a contract with the Witch, an enormous rift opened up in the streets, and I collapsed into a field of oil." I scratched my head. "Oil, fossil fuels, and coals. Those are all created through the remnants of plant and animal matter which form, uh, hydro . . . hydrocarbons. I don't know if it'll help me find the diamond blade, but if I manage to find more oil, maybe I'll at least be able to find the resources I need to heal my arm."

"Doesn't sound too far-fetched," Diana commented. I was surprised by how eager she was to go along with my idea and remembered what Grigory had said.

"Hey . . . you aren't going to join Grigory and that Pharaoh he says he's working for, are you?"

Diana shook her head. "As much as I think the modern generation is spoiled, I would never condone such destruction. In any case, this all shows that you inflicted serious damage to the boundaries of space-time when you pulled out the diamond blade. The God of Fire thrives amongst the chaos of the world, but one constant rule is that dead things are supposed to remain dead. With the ancient armies coming back and your ability to mutate your DNA through communicating with extinct species, the future might not look pretty for this world."

"Not pretty?" I muttered. "So does the planet, or the entire solar system, end up exploding if we use magic too often and can't seal the God of Fire?" I asked. "You're the four-thousand-year-old one, so you should have some memories, right?"

Diana sighed. "The world is a mysterious place," she said.

"There's no telling that the world *hasn't* been constantly in flux and reconfigured and that our memories haven't been altered to perceive a continuous world."

"Oh, so like the many-worlds theory of quantum mechanics when there has to be another world where the electron passes through the other slit . . . " I began. "Oh, never mind, I'm sure my feeble mind isn't enough to interpret advanced physics theories, let alone this magical world I got pulled into." I stood up to my feet and tried my best to stretch about. My stomach growled, and Diana pulled out some of the impala jerky she'd preserved yesterday.

"I'll get you to a freshwater source, as well," Diana said. My entire body ached as I followed Diana through the forest, dizzy and dehydrated from the battle against Grigory.

If a jaguar jumped out of the trees — hell, if I even just made a wild boar mad, I would probably die without Diana's help.

Once Diana led me to the small creek, I gulped up the flowing water ravenously. Within a few seconds, I began to regain my strength, and I dipped my infected arm into the water as well to attempt to wash off some of the grime. The purple veins bulged a bit less after washing, but I still didn't regain my right arm's functionality.

"Thank you," I said. "Now, shall we get going straight to this source of oil?"

"We've got no other clues, and we have to act fast," Diana said. "Both for the sake of this world's stability and for the sake of your infected arm."

"All right then, my piggy-pig nose will show us the way," I said as I took the lead and followed the scent toward the oil leakage.

It took another half-hour or so as we made our way through the winding forest, and I was looking forward to having a relatively peaceful day after the battle with Grigory when the trail ended on a steep cliff. Luckily, it seemed like there were an endless amount of platforms that looked like enormous Venus fly traps, and beneath those oversized plants were endless amounts of spiky stems and branches leading down to what appeared to be a muddy swamp.

"Well, you've really done it now," Diana said.

"Now what?" I grumbled as I looked at the oversized plants.

"Even the Witch of the Forest wasn't able to mutate plants *this* much," Diana said.

"So I made some plants bigger?" I asked. I hoped that these things only looked like Venus fly traps as a flock of carefree birds landed on one of the green platforms and began to suck at the delicious nectar available at the center . . .

Squawwk! Cawww! Only one of the birds was fast enough to escape and scatter as the Venus fly trap closed in and prepared to slowly digest the remaining four birds. I started to turn back, but Diana pulled at my arm.

"Trying to go around will take too long," Diana said decidedly. "You saw how far this cliff face stretches." I turned back and looked for a gentle incline on the cliff, but Diana appeared to read my mind and shook her head. "Jumping across the platforms is our best chance. There was a long delay before it closed in on the birds, and if we try to cross the swamp below, it's more likely than not we'll become crocodile food. We can't cross the vines and plant trunks either without getting impaled by hundreds of spikes."

"I can see the edges of the other cliff from here, but it still might take hundreds of these Venus platforms to cross over," I said. "Even if they react slowly on average . . ."

"So you'd rather go down to the swamp and hope that all the crocodiles you meet there are slower than the fastest plant?" Diana asked. I couldn't respond to that, and it seemed like Diana was adamant that jumping across the carnivorous plants was better than the swamp, the spiky vines, or trying to find a way around. "We also can't share the same platforms as they'll close after we touch them, but try to stay close to me."

"Will do," I said as Diana led the way on our next reckless adventure. The enormous Venus fly trap pressed down under her weight, and by timing her jump perfectly, she jumped forward just before the jaws of the plant closed. She'd used it like a trampoline to bounce from plant to plant. It appeared that she wasn't in the mood to look back, and so I followed suit to jump on the nearest plant platform.

After several jumps and a few close incidents with death, it finally felt like I was getting the perfect timing down. "Woohoo!" I declared as I bounced from plant to plant and soared through the air like a manic flea. This was the first fun thing that I'd come across since the truck hit me, even if I was still flirting with death. However, once I'd crossed a number of these Venus fly traps, I started to notice that the platforms became more awkwardly angled and more distant from each other. Diana was doing fine somehow as she jumped on ahead, but I was forced to take a left turn and tried to work out a new path. "I'll catch up to you soon!"

Just when it felt like I was finally making a good turn, I saw the plant walls around me suddenly begin to close. I didn't have time to spring off the platform and dove forward. The plant's jaws closed around my left ankle, but the rest of my body had escaped as I dangled awkwardly in the air. But there were no platforms I could land on from my current angle, so I would have to trust the spiky vines or the swamp below. "Diana!" I called out. I had to bite down the remnants of my pride. "A little help?" I didn't hear her call back and wondered if she was satisfied with letting such a pathetic hero die an early death. The Venus fly trap was confused that it had merely snagged onto an ankle, and its outer teeth-like spines struggled to pull me closer until it opened up once more. Apparently, it had decided to settle for unfortunate wandering birds.

"Aaaaah!" I yelled as I dropped straight toward the endless vines and branches. The spikes were as sharp and long as they appeared, but luckily, they didn't point straight upwards. My fall was somewhat broken by falling through a cluster of spiky vines and branches, and when I tried to secure my position by grabbing a branch, it only resulted in leaving nasty gashes on my palms and wrists. So I could only hope that the crocodiles waiting in the swamp would be extremely slow, and I wished there would be friendly swamp dolphins to assist me.

I fell into the murky swamp with a loud splash and desperately paddled upwards, and I hoped that the crocodiles here would confuse my appearance for a large rock. When I broke through the surface of the water, I paddled and looked around for dry land. There wasn't any in sight, but by a miracle, I found a shallow part of the swamp that only reached my waist after a couple of minutes. I looked up at the canopy of vines and oversized Venus fly traps above, and I found nothing that could serve as a convenient handhold. The spiky vines curved and twisted too often and created dead ends of spiky balls that were impossible to scale.

Think, Abyss, think.

If I'd transformed my right arm into a claw with talons during the fight with Grigory, perhaps I could do the same with both arms and even my feet in order to climb up one of these tree trunks. But I wasn't sure if my body was capable of doing such a thing, and even if it was, that would mean infecting and crippling all four of my limbs. I hoped Diana could quickly weave a rope ladder with all of these vines or summon some magical spell from her bags.

"Diana!" I yelled at the forest canopy above but received no reply. However, I noticed a moving log in the water, which bobbled toward me slowly. My worst fears came to fruition when the log bobbed upwards to reveal two voracious, reptilian golden eyes.

So this was nature, being predator one day and prey the next.

"Uh, Mr. Crocodile," I said. "Or Alligator, Altruistic Alligator? I'm not tasty at all. I don't have enough fat on me, and I've got far too many rib bones, in fact . . ."

Shrhruhsshshhh!

The crocodile bolted toward me with its jaw open, and I desperately tried to run with the water at my waist, pulling me backward. I think that I probably made three good steps before the crocodile snapped at my most exposed appendage, my unlucky left leg. Just as I felt the teeth of the creature's mouth begin to pierce my skin, I saw the shadows of rot and fossils of long-extinct creatures begin to swarm into my body. This was my power, and even if it was only capable of mutating one limb for a limited time, it would be enough to fend off this hungry crocodile.

Intense pain shot through my entire left ankle as it jolted upwards. I toppled backward and floated there as the crocodile roared in pain, the flesh of its mouth and jaw sent splattering by my new transformation.

"Arrrgh . . . take that, croc!" I yelled as I reoriented myself to inspect my new mutation. My left ankle had erupted into a large spiky ball like a porcupine, and I could see some of the diamond quills lodged in what remained of the crocodile's snout.

Three more floating logs approached to investigate the scene.

Please, let them just be floating logs . . .

As I attempted to awkwardly walk away from the scene, the three logs became a trio of voracious crocodiles who proceeded to cannibalize the one I'd just injured. Blood stained the swampy water as the animals ripped the creature apart limb by limb before finally turning to me. Their dinner was far from over, and it seemed like I was going to be an exotic dish on their menu despite my small size.

I could hardly move my left leg now that it had transformed. If I used the same porcupine mutation with my other body parts, I would be rendered immobile and stuck in this swamp for good, but it appeared to be my only option. Maybe I could bust out some new moves with my spiky left leg and die like an epic kung-fu fighter . . .

Thok.

An arrow sprouted from one of the crocodiles that surrounded me, and it awkwardly collapsed back into the swamp as if it had been hit by powerful poison.

Thok, thok.

The two remaining crocodiles fell unconscious, and my cheetah-cheeked guide swung down from the canopy with multiple spiky vines attached to her waist. Diana sighed as she cut the vines suspending her and dropped down next to me.

"You showed up just in time," I said as she quickly inspected my body. Even in the swampy water, the glint of the diamond quills that had erupted from my left ankle was visible.

"Mutation in swampy water. Your left ankle is going to *really* get infected," Diana said. "But before that, we need to find a way back up. Did you want to see the crocodiles that badly?"

"I had the worst luck when it came to landing on the one Venus fly trap that had a fast reaction time," I started. "And most likely, we'll have to climb the vines unless I can sprout wings with my power or something, right?"

Diana shook her head. "You're able to achieve many impressive things with your magic, but even if you mimicked the body structure of a bird, you wouldn't be able to carry my additional weight. But if you could just explode quills like that, maybe a sudden mutation on one limb would be enough to blast us back up toward the platforms above." Diana tied her bow behind her back and grabbed onto my shoulders from behind.

"Are you serious?" I asked, trying to hide my blush. Even if it was in the context of trying to survive an epic adventure, this was the first time a girl was willing to press her body against mine. I closed my eyes and tried to channel more of the energy from the thousands of species and organisms that had evolved in this swamp. Everything would be focused on my already mutated left leg, and I tried my best to imagine a coiled-up spring pushed down as far as possible. My muscles began to twist as they absorbed the dark oil, and I could feel the bones in my ankle violently shift again. The pain sent stars into my vision, and I almost passed out from the shock. If I'd tried to pull this off against the crocodiles, they would have ripped me apart before I could form the proper mutation.

"Hang in there, Abyss." Diana slapped my right cheek with one of her hands, and I finally found enough focus. I wasn't sure if I had the proper angle, but my muscles and bones had shifted into a coiled spring.

"Diamorph Leap!" I shouted as I released the coils within my left leg. I felt another immediate sharp burst of pain as Diana and I sailed up toward the canopy of spiky vines. It turned out that my face would take the majority of the blows, and as I'd exhausted my available mutation on my leg, no diamond padding would shield me as I sailed up toward the air with Diana. When I managed to open my eyes, the two of us landed on a Venus fly trap together.

As the carnivorous plant sunk under our weight, Diana pulled me up toward my feet, and I realized that my left leg was now completely dead weight. I would have to hop on my right leg until I made it to the other cliff-side. "Together this time!" Diana said as she made the jump. I hopped up just as the plant closed its hungry jaws. It missed me by a lucky two inches or so before I tumbled toward the next platform Diana prepared to land on. Miraculously, hopping on one leg was enough to make it through the Venus fly traps. The landing on the other side of the cliff was rough, and I ended up with a face full of dirt.

"God, I'm beat . . . " I said as I rolled over and looked up at the sky. My stomach was growling once again—it figured that sudden mutations required many calories to support the shift back into human. "I'd like some more impala jerky . . ."

"I dropped it all when you made that jump," Diana said bluntly. "I'll see what I can hunt on the other side of this cliff in the forest. It's probably best to set up camp for the night." I forced myself up, shook my head, and muttered curses under my breath. "What was that you said? Diamorph leap?"

"Well, it sounded cool enough, didn't it?" I asked. "All famous heroes in comic books have their signature moves, don't they?"

"Don't move too much and just rest," Diana said. "I don't know if your left ankle will be good by tomorrow, but from the look of it, any more traveling today will risk serious injury." When I looked down at my left ankle, I discovered that it was in far worse condition than my right arm. The muscles were still struggling to untwist themselves from having been winded into a coiled spring, and most of the infected warts were bleeding and oozing pus. There were a few hardened clumps of hair that had formed quills that were now in complete disarray and only served to worsen the pain and infection. It was an ugly sight that anyone suffering from the bubonic plague would envy, but luckily, it only affected my left ankle.

"I wish I could just be like rubber!" I yelled up to the sky, hoping that the Witch that I'd contracted with me would understand me.

"With no bones?" Diana asked. "Then you wouldn't be able to function unless you were in an aquatic environment like an octopus."

"Just get to hunting. I'll eat up an octorok if that's what it takes to heal my limbs," I said, with my stomach still growling. Diana again had the same puzzled expression on her face but understood that she wouldn't get the reference and headed out toward the forest.

I sighed as I leaned back and looked up at the sky. I had asked to be a hero on an adventure, but everything was so much cleaner in video games and comic books. The protagonist could just be an energetic and happy-go-lucky idiot who shrugged off doubts and fears because, in the end, some incident would happen, and he would be the only one who could save the day. But now, I was sent on a quest because I was the one who'd caused the problem by pulling out the diamond blade. And my weird power left my limbs looking like something out of an edgy horror movie. At the very least, I had Diana on my side with her impressive marksmanship, able to shoot down hungry crocodiles while she was suspended by spiky vines.

This is only the beginning. I shouldn't be too negative.

I would meet more allies to help me on the quest after Diana, and eventually, I would prove Simon and Justin wrong when I returned to the Western Sanctuary. I sat up and tried to practice simple boxing movements without using my legs. I probably looked like a fool, and I was lucky that no one was around. I wasn't sure if it was one or two hours, but Diana finally returned with an oversized rabbit in her hands as the sun began to set.

"You made all the wildlife go awry," Diana said, her face caked in sweat and exhaustion. "Everything in the following forest is weird. You'll see for yourself if you can walk tomorrow." The rabbit she'd hunted down was twice the size of a normal rabbit, and I noticed that it had three visible arrow wounds on its body. "It took me three shots to get this guy to slow down and stop, and when I pulled out my arrows, I noticed that its skin and muscle were both much thicker and tougher."

"But it's more food for both of us in the end, so worth it, right?" I asked. I still couldn't quite get the hang of using the bow and spinner, especially since I'd lost so much dexterity with my right hand.

Diana expertly got a small fire running again and grew it gently. She used a smaller supply of dry grasses and branches. My stomach continued to rumble as I watched my skewered rabbit meat slowly cook.

"Thanks a lot for everything, Diana. I would've just ended up a reject amongst the Witches' heroes if you hadn't come along and offered to train me. I still would've preferred more equipment and training, but an awesome guide works, as well. If there's any way I could repay you . . ."

"Just try not to fall down and almost get eaten by a crocodile again," Diana said quickly. Even if I wasn't so awkward, it wasn't easy to tell how to reply to a four-millennium-old hunter girl. She had her reasons when it came to keeping her distance. But to my surprise, she was mature enough to muse for a bit instead of letting herself ferment in a foul mood. "Maybe I'm the odd one out. Grigory—I still can't believe I'm calling him that—he always did seem quite bored of life in our little tribe. He would have become our chieftain if we'd been left to live in peace, but I wonder if he would have been satisfied with that. I should have gotten over him by now as he was my first crush, but I didn't think that I would have the opportunity to see him again."

I didn't know why I decided to run my mouth. "I don't want to pry, but I only saw part of your memories. I'm not exactly sure how the Pharaoh Sobekatoes . . . " I was pretty bad at remembering foreign names.

"All men are the same, aren't they?" Diana suddenly asked. "Either they end up as undesirable losers, slaves in ancient times and what you'd call couch potatoes in your era, or they end up so ambitious and competitive in their search for power."

I decided to take a bite out of the meat instead of replying, as I probably couldn't think up good responses on an empty stomach. It didn't taste significantly better or worse than the gazelle, but it was still too dry, and I wondered where the next available source of fresh water was. Diana appeared to sense my thirst and handed me a spiky, thick vine.

"Is this our best source of water?" I asked.

"There were no creeks or rivers up ahead, but we lucked out on these," she explained. "I have containers, too, and if it comes down to it, we can recycle our urine."

"Gather more of these vine things first thing in the morning then," I said as I took the knife Diana had lent me and cut open one end of the vine. The water inside was coated with bitter tree sap, but I forced it down my throat. I noticed that there was less of the rabbit meat than I had expected, and Diana shrugged. Had I really eaten so ravenously?

"We'll have less jerky to go around tomorrow," she said. "Transforming your leg into a quill-spitter and then a coiled spring must have taken a lot of energy that you need to refill on." Diana quickly jumped in, prepared a few extra strips of rabbit jerky, and handed the cleaner organs to me. "Make sure you cook them thoroughly. You can start on the bone marrow of the cooked parts now."

I had never enjoyed the taste of liver, and I wasn't looking forward to eating three to four times the amount that I usually ate. "Cartoon characters have it good when they can always find a restaurant and a chef to pig out on," I grumbled as I started smashing the rabbit bones. "Or hopefully, I could eventually evolve a multi-chambered stomach so I can graze for easy food sources, although that'd also mean regurgitating the plant matter and chewing the cud." I didn't really have time to attempt to make more small talk as I sucked out the marrow to the best of my ability. It wasn't anyone's idea of a romantic date, but Diana didn't look the least bit disgusted. Human beings were scavengers as well as hunter-gatherers at one point, and yet, as we became more civilized, we insisted on meaningless things like table etiquette.

Diana told me when the organs were done cooking and urged me to eat them up now, for it was much more difficult to preserve them. Despite my increased appetite, I still occasionally gagged at the taste of the roasted organs and grabbed an extra water vine to help wash it down.

"Good night, Diana." We hadn't really been able to set up a shelter, but I was far too tired to care by now. While I had thoughts of digging into a hamburger and fries as I drifted off to sleep, little did I know that my journeys ahead would contain far more unpleasant foods.

My left leg had healed enough for me to walk on it despite the pain and aching, but if it came to jumping, I would probably still rely on my right leg. Diana seemed to approve that I was now ready to head toward the next section of the odd forest, and after quickly drinking one of the water vines, I was to lead the way toward the quest objective. As I walked toward the field of trees, I quickly discovered what Diana meant when she said that everything was awry.

There was no ground beneath us at all but merely spherical clumps of soil about the size of a large bedroom. The whole intricate structure was supported by tree trunks growing in every direction, which formed narrow make-shift bridges between the dirt spheres. "The vines that I harvested probably keep the network of water flowing through these trees since there's no ground to absorb water from," Diana explained. "We can't just cut away vines left and right, since if we rip off a tree's source of water, it might shrivel and die and block our path forward."

It all made sense to me, but I found making progress across this new area frustrating and slow with my awkward left leg. Diana stepped ahead of me in order to be the vanguard and ended up helping me across the twists and turns in the branches. I probably would have fallen down and broken something had it not been for her help.

I wasn't sure how many hours had passed, but through the canopy above, the sun seemed pretty far up in the sky. "We're getting closer and closer to the gas leak, at least," I said. As embarrassing as it was to have Diana lead the way, today was going far smoother than yesterday. Even if it was a bit boring, I couldn't afford to put additional stress on my limbs by pulling off another Diamorph transformation.

It must have been around noon, for Diana started snacking on her preserved rabbit jerky, and my stomach began to growl and whine. I had no right to ask for more given that she'd hunted it and I'd consumed so much the other day. "Can we catch another rabbit?" I asked. "Maybe we can set up an easy trap somehow . . ."

"Everything in this area is too humid to start a fire with," Diana said. The sound of birds chirping could be heard above, and she shrugged. "If you find a nest full of eggs, you can eat them raw." It took another half an hour or so for Diana to catch me my lunch. Somehow her keen vision spotted a nest in the branches to the left of us, and the cheetah-cheeked girl quickly pulled out her bow and notched an arrow.

Screecheeie!

The mother bird chirped as Diana's arrow pierced one of its wings, sending it down to the unknown depths below. Diana climbed toward the nest, deftly raided it, and carried the eggs within her pouch's bag. "Only three," Diana said, willing for me to have two of the eggs while she would take one.

"Thanks a lot again," I said. I really wish I could cook these eggs and add some bacon or ketchup, but my stomach wasn't feeling picky. I grabbed another one of the water vines, cracked the eggs, and downed their contents, and luckily didn't swallow anything resembling a developing chick. Unfortunately, the eggs didn't provide any unexpected boost of energy, so I was still quite tired and weary as the day went on.

Diana didn't find another convenient nest to raid, and the inverted forest didn't end as we grew close to the source of my oil power. And overall, Diana was getting more and more tired of having to help me cross the awkward branches while my leg refused to heal. I might have impressed her the first day by hunting down the impala, but in these last two days, she was becoming tired of being assigned to train a hero who she had to constantly save.

I felt stupid and spoiled in this twist of dramatic irony. I'd wanted to go on an adventure, but I'd assumed it'd go smoothly with constant chase and fight sequences, and limitless energy and food to power me, and a group of friends and allies that would always cheer me on. But even if the world contained magic, plants and animals alike weren't just going to allow themselves to be farmed and eaten. Still, even if my story had to be a classy high fantasy, I at least wished that we could sing a merry song like in the *Lord of the Rings* to lift our spirits, but Diana wasn't even in the mood to do that.

The sun was beginning to set above us, and we were both tired from trekking and climbing all day, so Diana decided to set up camp. She was probably used to going without a meal or two, but my hunger made me surly and sullen. When we stopped, I started to sense something within the rotting tree trunk on my right. "This area seems to have been over-hydrated with these water vines, as the bark is way too soft, and . . . " Diana raised an eyebrow as I dug the stone knife into the soft tree trunk. When I stripped away the bark and layers of rotting wood inside, I saw seven large beetle larvae, each around six inches long. Unexpectedly disturbed, they were now writhing awkwardly.

"Abyss, you found us dinner," Diana said without a hint of sarcasm. "You can have the extra one since you're not done healing, are you?"

"You have the extra one," I started before my stomach interrupted me. "I owe you so much for what you've done, after all . . ."

"We'll split it," Diana said, causing me to blush awkwardly. She couldn't possibly mean that, could she? Instead of having a cute spaghetti kiss scene with a princess, I was going to have a larva-kiss scene with a wild hunter girl.

Diana looked at me like I was a moron, and I shrugged off the thought as I took my first beetle larva. "They really need seasoning to taste any good, but we don't have anything better," Diana said. "Along with scavenging, we often ate insects if we couldn't get enough food from the hunt, although it's rare to find grubs this big." Diana popped the larva into her mouth like it was cotton candy and quickly licked up the guts and blood that oozed out from her lips.

"Bottom's up," I said as I ate the larvae. It tasted as disgusting as it looked, but I knew that my stomach needed some sort of protein. If Grigory or Melosh or another crocodile popped up in front of me, I wanted to have some energy stored up. I wished that Simon had given me some toothpaste to wash away the bitter residue on my tongue as I ate my second and third grubs along with Diana. "Last one," I observed the seventh writhing grub.

"It's been a while, but I can make a pretty good split," Diana said as she picked up the grub and bit off its top half, guts and all, making a clean cut with her teeth. I was a bit disappointed that this was how splitting our meal would end up. Still, if I ate the grub, it would have some of her saliva still on it. The bottom half was still writhing despite the loss of its brain, and I took it and quickly popped it into my mouth, trying to savor any part of this indirect kiss. It tasted the same bitter, rancid flavor as the first three, and I almost laughed out loud at my own foolishness.

"My stomach's . . . a little less upset," I said. Even though we were both tired, it wasn't anything like the encounter with Grigory and the crocodile from yesterday, so a long and awkward silence passed between us. "Do you really have no interest in the modern world?" I asked. "Did you at least learn to read and write? I heard it's much harder from a certain age, but once you get it down, you'll discover more things than you'd thought were possible."

"It's all the same," Diana said. "In the last few centuries, they developed those things, right? Telescopes and microscopes, tools to see really far away and to see really small things? It's . . . it's fun at first, to be able to discover a new world, but sooner or later, you'll be burying your head in a textbook memorizing all of these arbitrary names and diagrams, right? Hoarding cocktails of drugs to live a few years longer."

"Okay then, fine," I said. "How about I try to tell you a famous story then? Although I'm not sure I'm able to remember even a dozen lines of iambic pentameter, so I wouldn't do Shakespeare much justice . . ."

"Don't parrot the tastes of some fancy critic," Diana said. "Tell me a fun story. What did you really mean when you said you wanted to be like rubber?"

I chuckled to myself. "Fine then, we'll tell the story of the most popular comic book in history so far." I probably would appear to be a total nerd if this was a normal date with a normal girl, but Diana wasn't picky. "Once upon a time, there was a boy named Luffy, who wanted to become a pirate so much that he stabbed himself under his left eye . . ."

Diana didn't tell me to stop, so I narrated the summary of *One Piece* for over an hour or so. I wanted to say that she was already half asleep, but she did chuckle every now and then and asked questions. "The god Enel had the funniest look on his face when he discovered his lightning Devil Fruit powers had no effect on Luffy . . ."

"You say that we're only one-fifth of the way there?" Diana asked.

"It ran for over thirty years," I said. "I didn't come close to keeping up with it all. And the anime had what you would call filler, so it's even longer . . ."

"Well, it's interesting how long an author can make his story these days," Diana said. "And how much time and energy consumers of such content are willing to invest. But if you expect to be able to gather a pirate crew or adventurers like in that story so easily just because you have fancy powers, you'd be out of luck. Good night, and good luck with your healing."

I didn't need Diana to tell me that. I would have been happier if I was just a side character that could provide strategy and comic relief—I certainly had the awkward personality and the shoddy luck to match Usopp, after all.

Another night passed without being able to peer into Diana's dreams and memories. I wondered how long it would really take to get her to open up and see me as more than just another young hero to train. If she left me for whatever reason, would I manage to find suitable friends and allies, or even enough food to fuel my Diamorph powers? When I got up the next morning, my left leg was almost back to normal functionality, although it was still covered in warts and scars. Diana didn't appear eager for me to continue my discussion of contemporary pop culture, so I let my sixth sense guide me toward where the oil field was located.

We climbed the inverted, twisted trees for another couple of hours or so, and finally, the terrain transformed into a vast and open grassy field. "We're almost there," I said. The smell of burning gas was growing stronger and stronger in my nostrils. "Once I absorb the oil and heal up, maybe we can get back to hunting impala." My stomach didn't take eating the grubs and raw eggs warmly, and we hadn't found a lucky breakfast to begin the day with. There was no visible indicator of the field of oil I needed to absorb, so I continued to lead the way with my sense of smell when suddenly a powerful gust of wind knocked me backward.

"Watch out!" Diana snapped out her bow and tried to look around at the target, but another gust of wind sent me sprawling across the soft grass and dirt.

"So this is who the Pharaoh is interested in? Pathetic. He told me that I was free to do as I pleased with the immortal hunter, though." A female voice rang through the air. As I looked around, I saw a tall, voluptuous woman in red and golden clothing was standing on a platform of swirling winds and clouds.

"She's one of Sobekhotep's concubines," Diana explained. "Although I don't quite remember her name . . ."

"Bethany will do as an English translation," the voluptuous woman said. "And you were one of the few concubines dumb enough to reject her good fortune, refusing to serve the great Pharaoh." Bethany was looking at Diana with spiteful eyes. "You even took the name Diana after the Roman goddess, in an attempt to reclaim your purity." Diana pointed her bow and arrow up at Bethany, but the floating concubine didn't flinch. "Your arrows will just be deflected by the wind, so don't bother, wench. I was the Pharaoh's favorite for well over a decade, but as soon as the smallest signs of age showed up on my face, he decided to toss me to the side for younger girls like you."

"Blame the Pharaoh then. I never volunteered to be part of his harem . . . " Diana started. A sharp gust of wind slashed across her cheek, and a small scar appeared seconds later.

"There's no need to get violent," I tried to speak up. "Diana's training me, and I just came here for the oil I need to absorb . . ."

"Step out of this, young one." Bethany then blasted me with a sharp gust of wind, which cut straight through my toga and formed a scar on my waist. "Because of Diana's actions, human progress has been delayed and marred by wars, famine, and disease in the last four thousand years. If our Pharaoh hadn't had the fruit of immortality stolen from him, he would have been able to advance civilization at a much more impressive rate. Now that his return is imminent, I was chosen to enact Diana's punishment." Bethany sent out three more gusts of winds, which scarred Diana's arms and left abdomen, and I gritted my teeth. I didn't know how to take down this new enemy.

"You're as petty as they come," Diana said as she shot out arrow after arrow against Bethany. But as the floating beauty had predicted, all of the arrows were easily deflected by gusts of wind. Diana's running only delayed her next wounds from the wind-blades, invisible air currents that moved too quickly to dodge.

Did I have any chance of reasoning with Bethany? I jumped at her repeatedly without any better ideas, and it appeared she was content to ignore me. I needed to at least shield Diana and repay her for everything she did for me. But the cheetah-cheeked hunter wasn't quite fond of that idea, and she continued to fire arrow after arrow in futility.

"You're just wasting ammo like this!" I shouted above the roar of the winds. "I'll handle it somehow!"

Bethany was amused by my attempts at playing hero. "You don't need her anymore, Abyss," the concubine said. "The Pharaoh will give you your next missions and train you well, feed you well, and provide you with girls that are much more beautiful."

I gritted my teeth and wracked my brain for ideas.

If I used a Diamorph transformation, it shouldn't kill me since I'm so close to the oil, which would heal me, but what could I do with that?

If I sprouted wings, I would just become light enough to be easily swatted away by Bethany's gusts of wind.

"Got to aim then," I said as I bent my knees and prepared to make another coil. Diana noticed my reckless attempt and ran over to my side, her arms full of dozens of cuts from Bethany's windy blades.

"You won't be able to hit her in your jump," Diana said. "If you can pull off another Diamorph move, use it to throw me toward her instead!"

"What?" I asked as my legs buckled under the pressure. My muscles were trying their best to re-form the coiled springs I'd used in the deadly swamps, but for some reason, my legs decided to rebel. Perhaps I really hadn't eaten enough.

"As long as I get within a certain range, I can guarantee a deadly hit with my magic," Diana said. She raised a leg as if willingly putting her ankle in my right hand, but the idea still seemed idiotic and gruesome.

"What about when you come *down*?!" I exclaimed. "There's no way I can catch you . . ."

Diana shrugged. "I'll likely die and wait for the next one or two people to come along and restore my body," she said. "All I know is that I'm not going to die from a concubine's petty attempt at revenge."

I tried to push my legs to transform for a few more seconds, but instead, the energy went toward my right arm, which had begun to become grotesquely muscular. Even if I consciously rejected Diana's idea, my unconscious body somehow knew that throwing her at Bethany was the best strategy. Bethany seemed to quickly deduce our plot and started sending gusts of wind at my augmented, throbbing arm. I started blacking out from the pain inside my body as well as the cuts from the outside, and Diana lightly tapped my cheek again.

"Throw me straight at Bethany," Diana insisted. "She'll try to deflect me as much as possible, but if you throw me with all the force you've got, I'll still get a solid hit in." I grabbed onto Diana's ankle with my oversized, muscular arm and stepped toward Bethany. The winds were still blasting at my face, but due to a combination of my increased weight and determination, it wasn't enough to break my focus.

"Diamorph . . . launch!" I yelled, hurling Diana toward the floating concubine. As soon as she'd left my grip, I regretted going along with such a foolhardy strategy. Bethany deflected the human projectile as predicted, but Diana was still skilled enough to whip out her bow mid-flight and let an arrow loose. The next thing I saw, a shaft sprouted right out of Bethany's left breast and had pierced deep enough to puncture her heart.

"You two, both such wretched fools!" Bethany cursed as the same purple-black gas started billowing out of her mortal wound. I was now focused on Diana, though, who was nearing the apex of her trajectory and would soon be hurtling downwards. The soft grass wouldn't be enough to break her fall, and she wasn't going to be lucky enough to have tree branches and leaves in this vast, open plain.

"Diana!" I yelled as I ran toward my falling mentor. There was no way I would be able to make it in time, but I desperately worked every muscle in my body. I couldn't immediately transform right after I'd buffed my arm strength, and the additional weight on one side was making my sprint incredibly awkward. If Diana died here, she would cause the death of at least one other person who wandered close enough, and then she would have the opportunity to revive. But I didn't want to drag any innocent people into this mess, even if that had been how it was for Diana many times over the course of her long life.

This is bad. I repeated the mantra in my head. Diana's head was almost going to hit the ground. I pushed myself into a futile dive at the last second, still several meters away from her, and the world began to spin in my eyes.

There was oil and fossilized remnants of the dead all over this battlefield, and they began to listen to my plea. The living creatures—gophers, spiders, earthworms, and ants all began to carry out the will of the undying and quickly transformed the ground, which Diana was going to break her bones on. The world continued to spin until I was suddenly seeing through Diana's eyes. I ascertained the patch of ground that needed to be morphed if she was to survive the fall.

Everything awkwardly turned into diamonds or muscles—my body couldn't produce more muscles at this point, so netting would have to do. It would save Diana's life, even if it made for an uncomfortable landing. The ground Diana was going to land on turned into an enormous hole in a split second, and the soil quickly transformed into thin strands of diamond netting. *More, more . . .* I pleaded with the living and dead creatures of the earth. More layers of netting, at least seven, at least eight . . .

Before I could determine whether or not Diana had been saved by the net, my consciousness returned to my body, still stuck in mid-dive.

Time passed very slowly for the world around me while my mind saw shadowy hands and fang-filled jaws begin to rise from the ground. I'd pushed my magical power to the brink in order to save Diana, and I would now face the consequences of doing something so ridiculous. My vision went black as I felt a vast sea of black oil wash over my body. My mind was no longer mine as the lust and fury of thousands of living things began to surround me.

Whether it was screeching, roaring, growling, or even clicking, dozens of animal minds were observing me like I was an endangered species at the zoo. The first thing that came back to my senses was my body, although there was still nothing but pitch-black oil around me. I was starting to gain my thoughts back as the animal sounds began to fade when suddenly, three rows of hungry fangs sunk into my left arm. I could feel my flesh being continuously ripped off as if there was an endless supply of muscle to feed on. When I attempted to scream, an animal jaw proceeded to crush my neck as well, and I tried to fight these mysterious creatures in sheer futility.

After a couple of minutes or so, the hungry jaws were finally satisfied with their meal of human flesh, and I was able to make words again. I was still sweating in dreaded horror. "What do all of you want?" Dozens of different animal eyeballs erupted from the black darkness, but none of the jaws from the past could vocalize. "Is this karma?" I asked. A long train of memories suddenly washed over me. I'd probably eaten hundreds of animals over the course of my short life and would continue to eat more of my fellow creatures in the future. "For the apex predator to be eaten alive, the species that was cruel enough to breed others for meat and slaughter?"

I heard some clicks in the black sphere of oil I was stuck in and then a few growls. Parts of my brain were being sucked out, unraveled like a bowl of fresh spaghetti so that these animals that observed me could manage to vocalize their thoughts and feelings through language.

"Food is life," I heard a voice reply to me. "Life is food."

"And for a long time, humans were food as well," I started. "Even today, the lucky crocodile or lion can eat up a full-course man . . ."

"Eight billion humans," the voice responded. "Destroyers. So many of us . . . *grrroarrr.*" The collective animal consciousness faded back into grunts and growls when emotions took over. Many of the creatures screamed in agony and fear upon recalling their deaths at the hands of human civilization. "Extinct, homes destroyed."

"I'm only one person," I insisted. "You won't get anything out of eating and torturing me in whatever dark pit you've trapped me in . . . " Before I could finish my thoughts, the jaws were at it again and clamped down on all four of my limbs this time. I still wasn't sure why I wasn't bleeding out and dying, and I wondered if my flesh was constantly being recycled with these fossilized creatures in this realm. It was basically the food chain sped up enough so that the animals became the legendary Ouroboros, which constantly ate its own tail.

"Food is life, life is food," the animal consciousness repeated. "Humans need food, but you have all of us now." The dozens of disembodied eyes seemed more curious than vengeful as they got a good taste of human. "Hero, work hard to save girl." The jaws gradually pulled away from ripping off my flesh, as if they allowed me time for one last comment.

"Did you guys create the diamond netting?" I asked. "Thanks for saving her."

"Work hard to save us, too," the animals insisted. Now that so many creatures had bit into my flesh in this dark realm, my muscles were learning new forms and new patterns to use in my next Diamorph transformations. "We become reborn. Then you keep our power."

I wasn't sure exactly what promises I could in fact carry out, since I still wasn't sure about the limits of my power. But it was like that in nature, too, wasn't it? DNA could acquire an endless array of mutations over time as species adapted to new environments and obstacles. I would need all the help that I could get in order to defeat Grigory, Melosh, and this mysterious Pharaoh who was returning from the dead.

Making a deal with a multitude of extinct animals that loved to chew on human flesh and bone seemed better than striking a deal with the Devil, at least.

"*Nrrargh!*" I heard Diana's groan as I went head-first into a patch of soft dirt. The dream that I'd been sent into felt too real, and my body remembered every inch of flesh in which the animals had eagerly sunk their teeth into. I pulled myself up to my knees and found that I was covered from head to toe in black mud. My right arm and my left leg were miraculously back to normal, however, and when I turned over to look at Diana, she was still in one piece despite having many bandages and scars on her arms.

"You're okay!" I exclaimed. I would have hugged her if I wasn't caked in the black mud, and Diana forced a weary smile.

"The netting you created was really impressive," she said. "But when I got here, you were stuck in the mud for almost two hours while I tried to pull you out. I figured it must just be the healing process after you discovered the patch of oil you needed, but you looked like an utter fool with your head and face in the mud like that."

"That was a great shot, sniping Bethany from mid-air," I said. "Is there any way you would be able to talk Grigory and that Pharaoh out of their . . . weird ambition, whatever it is?"

Diana's expression grew sour. "Yeah, about that. I would rather not talk so much about my past, and I'd rather you not pry, intentionally or not. You've learned a lot in three days, and you weren't the most annoying hero I was assigned with, but I've completed my duty." I wanted to protest that I would do more to help on our adventures next time, but Diana cut me off. "When I almost hit the ground, you hi-jacked my mind to see my landing, didn't you? Even if it was to save me, it was pretty uncomfortable. Like I said, I've given up on men, and there are plenty of girls both more beautiful and friendlier than me that you'll discover on your journey."

"I . . . who am I supposed to work with now?" I groaned.

"Two special agents have come here to assist you, since you pretty much just made reality even more unstable when you created the netting," Diana said. "I met them while you were stuck in the mud, and you should get along fine. Even if you don't, with your Diamorph powers, you'll definitely be able to survive the dangers of the world."

"And you're going to go back to your normal life?" I asked. I could see that it was hard for Diana to sympathize, given her age and experience, while the past week had completely immersed me in a new world of adventure. "I don't exactly know what's going on, but don't you think that you should at least try to save the world?"

Diana didn't budge. "If I come along with you, it might jeopardize the stability of the world even more if you keep trying to save me. We'd probably be playing right into the Pharaoh's hands. Although I guess I could drop a bit more advice. I don't know the limits of your Diamorph transformation, but if you want to stay healthy while foraging, stick to eating meats and fruits, as it's difficult for even experienced gatherers to determine which mushrooms and leaves are poisonous."

I wanted to protest further, but I also didn't want to appear pathetic, so Diana started to walk away from me as she trekked across the grassy plains. I could hardly walk and was still hungry. I decided to stay in place to wait for the two special agents that Diana had mentioned.

Real life could never be as convenient as in stories, right? Not only did I have a rough time at the Western Sanctuary, but Diana had to consider me like a boss might treat a new intern—even if it wasn't as awkward as talking to normal girls, I wasn't worth much of her attention. The best thing I could do was cross my fingers and hope that I could see the friendlier version of her in my dreams again.

"Inder, he's finally out of his nap in the mud!" A young boy's voice came from my left. I turned to see a short boy with spiky blue hair and two knives strapped to his side. Trailing behind him was a fair-skinned girl with similar blue hair and a gentle smile. Even if she wasn't dressed in the clothing of a princess, this girl was definitely more along the lines of what one would expect from a love interest. While she wasn't as voluptuous as Bethany, her body still had more curves than Diana's, and she was slightly taller, as well.

"You can wash off in a creek if you'd like," the girl started. "I'm Inder, and this is Latis. We're half-siblings, and we've always been called to action when reality becomes unstable." Upon closer inspection, I could see that Latis was a couple inches shorter than me, finally making me feel a bit better about my own short stature.

"Nice to meet you," I said. "I'm Abyss, and apparently, Diana just decided that she was done with training me." I scratched my head, as I wanted to be honest, but I also tried not to look like a complete fool. "I pulled out the diamond blade, but that was only once. And apparently, my magic allows me to manipulate my body parts. So far, I've created a claw for close quarters, an awkward spring for jumping, and huge muscles when I threw Diana. And then I created netting somehow to save her, even though she didn't want me to. I want to think that it was just a dream, but whenever my power activates, I end up communing with a lot of extinct animals or something."

"That's pretty cool," Latis said. "The two of us are ice mages, but we're both a bit unusual." Latis took out one of his knives and began juggling and spinning it in his right hand. "Inder can create objects up to her own mass from thin air and freeze the ground and liquids with her abilities, but she's pretty clumsy when it comes to actual combat. On the other hand, I can only manipulate the water and ice structures inside my own body, but as you can see, I can push my athleticism above and beyond." Latis jumped high into the air and did three back-flips before he landed with the grace of a cat.

"Let's get you into the nearby creek," Inder said as she took one of my muddy arms without hesitation. "We didn't really pack extra clothing, but since it's pretty warm, you'll dry off quickly."

"So where to now?" I asked as I let Inder lead me toward my make-shift bath. "Diana just told me that I would be going around looking for oil fields to increase my power until I could finally wield the diamond blade once again and seal the Fire god or something. And nobody even really explained how this Witch-magic works, although I'm not sure I could understand more than the very basics of it."

"And your journey will probably continue like that," Inder said. Latis didn't seem to have anything to respond with.

"Will I at least be able to meet that legendary Witch that I contracted with and have her hand out a field manual?" I asked.

"I . . . we're all not supposed to talk too much about her," Inder said. "She was too powerful from the very beginning, so if she even learned the truth about the world and what she could really do, it might just make things worse. We purposely placed her in the peaceful suburbs so that she would be a last resort, an ace up our sleeve if the clerics and priests pulled off something reckless."

"What about the Witches that you two contracted with?" I remembered Sonny's story and how I hadn't really gotten to know many other heroes at the Western Sanctuary.

"Oh, we didn't contract with Witches," Latis said. "Would you believe it if we were the direct descendants of a god?"

"Latis, you aren't supposed to talk about Dad," Inder said. "If you're this rebellious at eleven, I really don't want to be with you when you turn thirteen."

"Ah," I said. "So at least you guys aren't four millennia old like Diana . . . right?"

Inder nodded. "I'm thirteen, right about your age."

"I just hope that Abyss can keep up with me, unlike the other heroes," Latis said with a smirk. I definitely couldn't refine my Diamorph enough to do a triple backflip like Latis, and I wondered what else he had up his sleeve.

"I don't sense any new oil fields popping up," I started. "Does that mean that we're just going to be hiking randomly until I need another sudden mutation, which will then direct me to the next field?"

"Sounds pretty good to me," Latis said. Once again faced with a weird and preposterous reality, I wished that I was a video game character and that my quest would be as simple as hunting for sacred stones and medallions.

CHAPTER FOUR

The dip into the creek got most of the black mud off of me, and adding to today's good fortune, Inder had actually brought a packed lunch. Now I wouldn't have to chase down another impala or settle for raw eggs and writhing grubs for protein. "It's just sandwiches," Inder said as she brought out the wrapped items from her bag.

"Sounds delicious," I said as I let the afternoon sun dry off my wet hair. I hadn't been given another set of clothes, but the set that the Western Sanctuary had given me was tough enough to endure months of wear and tear, and the water had gotten most of the oil off of my clothing, as well. "If you could find us some side quests . . . short odd jobs or whatever so that we could earn money and actually stop at restaurants . . ."

Inder shook her head. "Well, ever since you pulled out the diamond blade, wildlife, in general, has increased, and from what I've heard, more souls have been reincarnated when you created that diamond netting."

"So I should savor whatever sandwiches you brought with you . . . " I said as I began to unwrap my sandwich. Even though I said that I probably finished the thing in a couple of minutes due to my hunger. Mustard, mayonnaise, and pickles tasted like heavenly spices paired with the cold meat, and it was my best meal in over three days. My stomach wasn't as grateful, however, and I knew that I needed to eat more to compensate for my Diamorph transformations.

"So Diana wasn't exaggerating when it came to your

appetite," Inder said. She let me have another sandwich. Latis had also eaten quickly and was getting impatient while he practiced knife swings at a nearby tree.

"Are you two really half-god, though?" I asked. "Could we be living in a world full of demigods?"

Inder shook her head. "We can't say too much about our father, but the God of Fire isn't similar to Zeus when it comes to his descendants. Since the gods are an abstract concept, they don't have human desires or the behaviors of any other species. Well, since the God of Fire is chaos, he, or she, or whatever gender it chooses to be at the time, is capable of acting with human spontaneity, but whatever happens to their children isn't of their concern."

"But in a sense, scientific laws still apply to this universe even if magic temporarily bends and breaks physics somehow, right?" I wondered. "So, on other planets, could the gods have also made pranks and contracts with aliens and mate with them, as well?"

Inder smiled. "If you're so curious, you can just try asking those things to the God of Fire when you meet him. You'll probably just come away with more questions in the end."

"Enough chatter," Latis yelled as he pointed a knife in my direction. "I want to see what the hero who contracted with the legendary Witch is made of!"

I finished the bites of my sandwich and rose to my feet. "I do need to get stronger, one way or another," I said.

Inder used her ice magic to form two dull *blades* for Latis and one stick the length of a sword for me. If I wanted to defeat Grigory and even stronger opponents, I would have to train when I wasn't foraging for food and hunting.

"Latis, go easy on him," Inder said. "You do remember what happened with Nole, didn't you?"

"He's got unbreakable bones," Latis said. "I've got to give him one-hundred-and-ten percent to awaken his secret power." Latis agreed to use the dull blades that Inder had given him, but I quickly learned that he meant what he said.

Despite my best efforts to block with the *sword* I was given, Latis pummeled me with dozens of strikes within our first minute of training. If he'd been wielding his real knives, my chest and stomach would have been turned into small meat cubes.

"Come on, Abyss, that all you got?" Latis finished off his combo string with a powerful forward kick and sent me toppling backward onto the soft grass. It was as embarrassing as getting perfected in a fighting game, and in addition, I was fully equipped with a new set of bruises and sore muscles.

"It's as brutal as any hero's training, I guess," I said as I forced myself back up. I wondered about the limits of my Diamorph powers. Could I have the thick hide of a hippo or the speed and reflexes of a mongoose?

Two more sparring sessions with Latis gave me the same result, and a look of boredom began to spread across his face. I was aching all over, but the fights against Simon and Grigory had built up tolerance.

"You've got endurance for sure," Latis said as he readied his dull blades once more.

I estimated over an hour passed of the spiky-haired boy covering my body in new bruises. I came close to landing a blow with my stick a few times, but Latis would always manage to dodge at the last second. Finally, I decided to throw away my sword, and Latis raised an eyebrow at me.

"My weapon is taking away the focus from my body," I decided. "You can keep your knives, Latis." Latis decided that he would fight bare-handed, as well.

It was always so easy in books and movies. A time-skip of harsh training could be described within a few paragraphs or a few minutes while inspirational background music played. But it was moments like these that were truly underappreciated, where I would probably have to spend the entire day training to get closer to Latis' level. I wanted to do my best now that I'd been given my opportunity to save the world and the universe, as bizarre as it was, and I wanted to be able to help Diana, as well. Perhaps it was just more delirium from the pain and soreness, but shadows began to form in the corners of my eyes.

Time itself was an illusion, wasn't it?

The crows and flocks of geese that would occasionally fly by overhead weren't always majestic and had started as ugly, bald hatchlings within their mother's nest. How many of them were only able to survive because they pushed their siblings out of the nest for food, and how many more of them had miraculously survived against their larger siblings and forced their mother to continue feeding them?

"Something weird's going on in your body, isn't it?" Latis asked as we began our boxing session. Even when it came to punches, I couldn't see and block most of Latis' attacks, but he was amused by how quickly I attempted to counter them. "Your pain tolerance is unreal, and you're getting a bit faster with every punch . . . " Even if Latis showed more caution this time, it wasn't enough for me to land a solid hit on him. The best I could do was the occasional glancing blow across his side as he bobbed and weaved gracefully. "I suppose you'll have to show me your power another time, Abyss." Latis hit me with two more hard punches, and finally, I reached my pain threshold.

I remembered how I'd broken down while a crowd gathered around me after my first defeat when I fought with Simon. I wondered if Justin, Sonny, and everyone at the Western Sanctuary still cursed me for pulling out the diamond blade, even if it had saved them from those clerics. I didn't know if it was psychologically healthy, but my newfound determination had an ugly lust for power to it, as well. Was it even possible for me to fight against Grigory and the Pharaoh without playing into their hands? Heroes defeated villains, at least most of the time, but what was the end result? A peaceful city or actually producing the greatest villain ever, having motivated him by weeding out the weaker criminals?

"You did great." Inder's reassuring smile brought me back to my senses. "A lot of heroes we worked with used their magic to try and avoid everything, but it's the first time I've seen someone just take so many hits from Latis." Even though it wasn't quite the desired compliment, I was glad that I finally had a supportive ally.

Latis chuckled. "I wish that I had grown up with you instead of the other kids at the orphanage. Well, I hope our mission can last at least a few years because I don't want to have to work with another wimpy hero."

"We're going to run out of sandwiches tonight," Inder said as she turned to me. "We can try to hunt down grazing animals tomorrow, but . . . since you created the diamond netting, Abyss, they've grown much faster and stronger, even birds and insects. Hunting really will not be easy, even if we all work together."

"It'll be fine," Latis said. "Abyss can recover and create his own armor with his Diamorph transformation, and all it'll take is for me to sneak up from behind and slit the throat." I couldn't think of a better hunting strategy as I finished my evening sandwich and began to drift off into sleep.

When I awoke, my body was still sore from yesterday's rough training. Latis didn't seem to pay it any mind, while Inder just flashed me another one of her encouraging smiles. The three of us all drank from the nearby creek and stored up some water before heading out toward the vast fields. The further we got from our creek, the taller and taller the grass seemed to grow, and the thin blades of orange and yellow almost reached my chin.

"It's going to be pretty easy to get lost like this," I said to Inder and Latis.

"On the bright side, it's much easier to hide," Latis said. Inder had attached a frozen blade to a tree branch, which would function just as well as the spear Diana had given me earlier.

It took a few minutes of hiking, but we finally noticed a herd of five impalas grazing on the grass. "All right, Abyss, just go distract him."

Before I could protest, Latis had already sneaked off to my right, his half-sister having not bothered to stop him. I approached the impala slowly and noticed that it seemed far more confident than the first one I'd hunted down. The creature appeared certain that it could bowl me over if I tried to attack, and it stood its ground as I got closer and closer. I had no idea where Latis would strike from. I wondered if I could simply buff up my arm enough to throw my projectile at a deadly velocity. And so, I stared down my prey for a few more seconds as the limbs in my body refused to mutate.

"Got ya!" Latis declared as he sprung out from behind. He jumped onto the impala's back and made a swift gash across its throat. The creature buckled back and threw the spiky-haired boy to the side, and as I saw the slight trickle of blood flow from its wound, I noticed its source of confidence. Latis' blade had only managed to penetrate into the impala's outer skin, as its vital arteries were shielded by tough fur and thick skin.

"So it's a challenge then!" Latis exclaimed as the impala rushed at him head-first.

Latis grinned with his knives ready and quickly adjusted his body to dodge the charge. But his prey was faster and tumbled sideways in mid-air in an abrupt, unnatural motion. With a thrust of its front legs, it caught Latis with a powerful kick, and I heard an unpleasant snapping noise as he tumbled across the ground.

"Latis!" I exclaimed.

"Don't let him get away!" Latis got to one knee and threw one of his knives at the impala — the target was hit in the right abdomen. I could see his left arm was dangling in its socket as he stood up, and I turned back toward the impala, which had bounded across the tall grass. It quickly became strands of brown fur floating above the grass, and I decided to heed Latis' words. If my sixth sense was still working, I could tire out the impala as it tried to flee.

Jogging was difficult, given my soreness from yesterday's training, and Latis was quick to complain as he followed my lead. Inder had been completely lost in the tall grass behind us, but Latis was much more focused on the hunt than his half-sister. "It's not my fault my Diamorph power won't just grant me cheetah or ostrich legs!" I said as Latis moaned and grumbled.

"Well, you're nothing but a common foot soldier if you can't jog faster!" Latis complained as he stepped in front of me once again and attempted to scan the horizon. "What's your sixth sense say?"

"When you keep interrupting me like that, I can't focus on our prey's thoughts," I said as I shut out Latis' words and focused on the wounded impala's *echoes*. Now that I'd established the mental link, I found that the creature's brain chemistry, as well as its physiology, differed from the first prey I hunted. There was less abrupt fear and panic and more aggression and anger, more frustration. "This way," I said as I turned to the right slightly and resumed jogging.

I was beginning to regret having trained so hard yesterday as the minutes turned into hours, and my face and shirt became caked in sweat. Latis was more outright about his disappointment in me than Diana had been. "Move it, Abyss!" he barked as I almost stumbled from exhaustion and soreness.

·"Or I'll take all the meat off the impala for myself, and you'll just have the bones!"

"I doubt you can eat that much without rupturing your stomach," I grumbled, but I knew that Latis was probably capable of beating me up with one arm. I could sense less and less aggression from the impala now and more desperation. Even if the wounds Latis had made weren't deep, the creature was still losing blood as it continued running from us.

The sun was high in the sky when we finally reached our collapsed prey, and my ankles seemed pounded by dozens of hammers. The air scraped and bit against my lungs, and it felt like I was receiving less oxygen to the brain, as well. "Well, we might as well work on your running as well as your fighting skills," Latis said as he reached the fallen creature and drew one of his knives. "I just didn't stab hard enough last time." The spiky-haired boy gripped his blade and thrust it into the impala's neck. Curiously enough, even with a better angle, the knife hadn't penetrated to the hilt, and Latis seemed to struggle as he cut past skin and muscle and severed the creature's vital arteries.

"What are we going to do about your arm?" I asked. "I don't know if we could go back to the Western Sanctuary, but there was a girl there who could brew up some healing potions."

"It's going to be . . . " Latis jumped to his feet before he could finish his sentence, and I noticed that we were surrounded by a group of six men, all readily equipped with swords and spears.

"We've found ourselves a good meal," one of the men started.

"Get away from our kill," I said, trying to appear confident. These men's clothing didn't seem to feature any symbols or patterns on them, so I couldn't tell if they belonged to the clerics that Melosh led or worked for the undead Pharaoh. They were shorter and leaner but had rugged and experienced faces that showed they were ready for brutal violence and deception.

"We're bandits and have only ever needed to respect force." Latis was already in a fighting stance, and as one of the men lunged toward him, he made his move. The spiky-haired boy stabbed the bandit in the thigh and caught his chin with a high kick—but as Latis was suspended in mid-air, another bandit quickly rushed in with his spear and intercepted his landing with a swift stab. Latis was writhing and struggling as two of the bandits pinned him down with their knees. He'd managed to knock the first foe out cold, which was probably going to be anything better than I could manage.

I remembered how badly my fight against Grigory had gone, and my stomach churned at the thought of another incident like that. Did I really have to be badly beaten and on the brink of death to awaken my powers? I was already exhausted from chasing the impala down, so I hoped that I could transform sooner rather than later. The leader of the bandits stepped toward me confidently, ready to slice me in two with his blade if I stepped out of line. "You'd really kill two boys over a dead impala?" I asked.

"Food has become harder and harder to capture," the bandit began. "It's like this in the animal kingdom, too, isn't it? Even if the cheetah does the actual hunting, a pack of hungry hyenas can step in and steal the kill. You stole the impala's life, and now we're just stealing food from another thief."

"You wouldn't want to push my limits," I said, and I decided to exaggerate my previous feats. "I fought off a crocodile and ripped off a man's arm."

Some of the men laughed, but the leading bandit could see the honesty in my eyes.

"Show them what you've got, Abyss," Latis grumbled under the weight of the two men. The bandit hesitated either due to curiosity or sympathy for my situation, and his first sword swing was slow enough to react to. *Good, make him think that I'm open, just like the impala, and . . .*

Twisting my body as I dodged, I jumped sideways and sprung out with a powerful front kick. The blow caught the bandit straight in the chest, and I felt something in my own leg crack as I awkwardly landed on my left leg. The three other bandits rushed in, and I knew that I could only hope to run from here. But my muscles had already reached their limits, and I felt no Diamorph transformation coming to save me this time. I twisted and turned and managed to dodge the first spear thrust just enough so that it grazed my left bicep instead of skewering my chest, but my luck was quickly dropping to zero . . .

Thok. Thok.

Two arrows sprouted from the men closest to me, and a third shaft sprouted from the remaining one. "Diana?" I exclaimed as I heard the galloping of a few horses.

"The warlords are here!" I heard the bandits exclaim as the three uninjured bandits tried their best to flee. They were all quickly mowed down by a shower of arrows, and as I turned to examine my surroundings nervously, one of the riders appeared next to me. I'd really hoped that it had just been Diana, and now I could only hope that there wasn't a third faction in addition to the clerics and the Pharaoh that I would have to deal with.

"I'm Oljatu, now-resurrected khan of the Jalair tribe," the man introduced himself as he stepped off his horse. He wore a blue tunic with a sword strapped to his side and a quiver on his back. The rider tied his black hair up in a ponytail, wore an old scar to decorate his right cheek, and appeared to be in his early thirties. "A mighty fine hunt you two boys have found today, although you could have done a much better job with protecting your spoils."

Latis grimaced as he readied his knife again, ignoring the

new gash in his right side.

"Put your weapons down, little one. I have come here to see that my distant descendant will continue his lineage."

"Wow, that's pretty cool." I turned to Latis. "So you're the son of a god and the descendant of an ancient warlord on the grasslands?"

"You are the descendant I was waiting for, not the spiky-haired boy," Oljatu corrected. I looked around to see if a third person had joined the scene, and with nobody else in sight, it appeared Oljatu really meant me. "You pulled out the diamond blade, did you not? And you even disrupted the boundaries between time and death even further when you reached your first power spring."

"I . . . " I began. "I was just doing that to protect the Western Sanctuary, even though they hated me. And I sort of fell into oil on that first quest of mine. I just pushed my powers to save Diana since she'd mentored me . . . " My stomach interrupted both the conversation and my train of thought with a loud growl, and Oljatu grinned.

"There is much for us to discuss and much for you to learn, young one," Oljatu said. "But first, it would do good to have some food in your belly, won't it? We'll lead you to our settlement." Oljatu gestured for me to get on his horse with him, and another one of the tribal warriors helped Latis onto his back. The tribesmen quickly stripped the meat and useful organs from the dead impala and carried it in large bags, leaving the bones and digestive tract behind. "What's your name?"

"Abyss," I said as I awkwardly climbed onto the horse behind Oljatu. "I don't remember any great warlord in my family history, but there are hundreds of thousands of men that are descendants of Genghis Khan, are there not?"

"Ah, it's a bit more than just the bloodline." Oljatu spurred his horse.

I held onto his waist as best as I could, but given my sheer inexperience riding a horse, it was still an uncomfortably bumpy ride. The galloping and constant vibrations made further conversations difficult until we reached Oljatu's camp. Luckily, it only took several minutes to find a special clearing in the tall grass. Including the riders that had come out to greet us, I counted around thirteen people in this resurrected tribe, all living in small tents alongside a crew of domesticated yak and sheep.

"Thanks for saving me, Oljatu," I said to the resurrected khan as our hunted impala was set over the fireplace. "But I really never thought of becoming a warlord or resurrecting my warlord ancestors." I scratched my head. "Sure, people remember Genghis Khan and Alexander the Great for being accomplished military leaders, but it's pretty unfair to the foot soldiers, let alone the widows and orphans that survived. In addition, even if culture and technology spread through military conquest, well, uh . . . flourishing, peace, and stability are never guaranteed. So in the end, we don't know whether or not lives are saved or improved . . ."

Oljatu flashed me a hearty grin. "My descendant, you're quite over-thinking things, aren't you?"

I looked at the crackling fire for more ideas and couldn't find a clever lie. "Things are just getting too weird around here," I said. "I don't know how you were raised or how you grew up, but if you were reborn in this era, wouldn't you at least try to enjoy the modern world before starting up your path of conquest? It's not like you can get very far unless you have magic. I mean, most bigger countries have guns and explosives and can even blow up large swaths of land from above. There's no way that archers on horseback can get much done, no matter how skilled . . ."

"But is that what you really want of the world, Abyss?" Oljatu asked. "A world so confined that men are locked up with their machines for both labor and entertainment and when war can be decided by a few deadly explosives?" Now Oljatu was sounding a bit like Diana.

"Swords, shields, spears, and bows are only fun in fantasy novels and video games," I said. "I don't know what I have to do to seal the God of Fire and meet the Witch I contracted with, but if I have to raid and pillage villages, I won't ever be able to see myself as a hero."

Oljatu snorted and looked at me as if he was dumbfounded at my lack of ambition. "Let's just say you're a work in progress," Oljatu decided.

I sighed. "The Witches possess magic in order to save humanity from its own violence, I was told. Surely the God of Fire must just be messing with us." I didn't want to say anything that would make my revived ancestor angry, and I wondered if he would see corporal punishment as fitting if I screwed up somewhere. I'd initially thought that Diana had been too cold to me, but other than Inder, she'd been the friendliest guide I'd gotten ever since I left the Western Sanctuary.

The impala meat cooked a bit faster than I had anticipated, and I eagerly munched on it, satisfied with the few spices that the Jalair tribe could spare. While it wasn't as good as the sandwich, it was much better than the raw eggs and beetle larvae that I'd dined on with Diana the other day. I remembered the Pharaoh's words when I'd visited Diana's dreams, and I decided to risk another query with Oljatu.

"Do you believe in something like Valhalla?" I asked him. "A paradise where warriors go to if they proudly died on the battlefield?"

Oljatu rubbed his chin. "Not quite, and neither do most of us herdsmen. Even in your modern era with your comfort and conveniences, medicines and delicacies, you folk still pine for heaven and hell, don't you?"

"I . . . was never that religious." I found my voice was trailing off.

"If you see no need for fighting, what do you think of marrying into our tribe?" Oljatu asked. "Rutyll is the most beautiful and responsible of us all, and when she died in her original life, she was still waiting for a husband."

"I'm, uh, only thirteen," I started. I thought of Diana when Oljatu brought up his suggestion. Even with her short-cropped hair, her lined cheeks, and the short duration we'd spent together, Diana had made quite an impression on me.

"An old enough age as any in most of history," Oljatu said, unfazed by modern sensibilities. "My brothers had marriages arranged at nine and ten." When he saw that my expression hadn't changed, he shrugged. "We have quite a long way to go with you, Abyss. After you finish lunch, why don't you try milking some of the yaks or shearing some of the sheep?"

"I'll give it a go," I said. "But I also do want to become a better fighter in general." I doubted that I could improve too much, but I didn't want to be humiliated like I had been in the fights against Simon and Grigory.

In total, I ended up spending at least a couple of hours doing herding chores with the other tribesmen. Perhaps a part of me should be glad that it was just tedious and tiring and not quite deadly, but it still didn't fit quite what I'd ever wanted in an adventure. Stripping off meat and flesh was one thing, but constantly milking the yaks' udders made the whole success of the dairy industry seem quite bizarre. "The first person to think of milking animals and making cheese must have been really hungry," I muttered to myself. As the milk began to dry on my hands, I once again realized that running water wasn't available.

Before I could go off and spar with Latis or any of the tribesmen, however, I ended up meeting Rutyll, the girl that Oljatu had suggested I marry. She wasn't particularly more beautiful than Diana, and although she didn't seem to have the abrasive personality that my cheetah-cheeked mentor possessed, the bigger problem was that she seemed to lack a personality at all.

"Are you fine with just doing chores again, even in your second chance at life?" I asked Rutyll.

Rutyll shrugged. She seemed to have been deprived of all opinions from growing up on these rough grasslands, perhaps only raised to serve her future husband — or perhaps even prepared to be kidnapped by a rival tribe in battle and become a slave? Girls at school could often be annoying with their gossip and rumors, but this was the other extreme.

"The herds are still pushed away by that horned monstrosity," one of Oljatu's men returned from the outer grasslands as he rode a horse. "Its hide is too thick to be penetrated by our arrows and spears. If we want to move our settlement, we'll likely have to loop far around its territory."

Oljatu scratched his head, annoyed. "What a pain. As long as that thing is up and roaming about, we can't engage in warfare with the neighboring tribes either." He then turned toward my direction and seemed to have a new idea fall into his head. "Why don't you make yourself useful again, Abyss? See what you can do about the horned beast."

"What can I do?" I asked. So far, my Diamorph transformations had allowed me to augment and harden my muscles, but did Oljatu just expect me to begin talking to troublesome animals? Granted, I had that weird experience where I fell into the oil pit to save Diana, but it wasn't enough for me to enter the situation with any confidence. I turned back at Rutyll, and it didn't seem like she cared whether or not I somehow defeated this horned beast or if I was ripped apart in a bloody battle.

Sutoff, the tribesman who'd reported to Oljatu was leading

me to the area where this horned beast dwelled. At first, I'd expected to see some sort of mutated monster with tentacles, spikes, and warts covering its body. Instead, I came upon a creature that looked mostly like a medium-sized horse, but with the deadly curved horns of a ram sprouting from each side of its skull.

"We predict that the disruption you caused in space-time didn't merely cause humans to jump back into existence from the dead, but it also may have created mutated animals from the many fossils of extinct species."

"What the heck does Oljatu want me to do with this guy?" I grumbled. "Maybe our best option would be to poison the grass around it and hope it ingests it and dies? You said his hide was too thick to damage from the outside, right?"

Sutoff just looked at me like my idea was as good as any, and so I inched forward cautiously in a half-squat to stay hidden in the tall grass. The ibex-horse hybrid was peacefully grazing the fields like any other herbivore and snorted as if mildly annoyed. He had definitely noticed me, but he probably thought that I was small enough to ignore. The horned beast definitely was six times heavier than me and would break half of my ribs with a half-assed kick.

So perhaps my best bet was to try and hope the creature could speak English after all then. "I'm Abyss, and here on account of the Jalair tribe. Would you consider temporarily leaving your territory so that they could cross . . . " Bad idea. The ibex-horse hybrid galloped up to me slowly, as if more amused and curious than aggressive. All I could do now was bluff and exaggerate my power, right? "I can make any part of my body as hard as diamond, so you better watch out . . ."

Clopcck!

The ibex-horse hybrid smashed his horns against my forehead, and I saw stars and lights as I tumbled backward onto the soft grass. As the static left my ears, I could hear the ibex snorting once more, almost as if it was chuckling at my resistance. He could never laugh as a hyena could, but I could definitely sense his emotions. As I rubbed my forehead, I found that there was miraculously very little blood, as if the Diamorph transformation had protected the front of my skull just enough.

"I'll get even harder next time," I claimed. "Since I introduced myself, who are you, exactly? I don't suppose you have a name, even in grunts and clicks?" I tried to click much like a whale or dolphin might, and I saw the horse-ibex seemed to smile in amusement. "How about I call you Ibonus?" Since the creature didn't object, it didn't seem to be a bad name. "I was just thinking of Epona, but you're a male ibex-thing, aren't you?"

Ibonus charged at me yet again, and I stood my ground, putting my faith in the Diamorph hardening. But this time, he stopped and just gently tapped my skull with one of his horns. "That's better," I started. I knew that I was still on thin ice when it came to trying to tame this wild animal. "Now, I know that this might sound crazy, but if I'm really destined to be a hero, I could ride you far away on my quests—and if you have the energy, you can carry a second passenger, too." Ibonus backed away as if he somewhat understood my suggestion. "I won't force horseshoes on you or slice you with spurs, but it would make things a lot easier for me . . ."

Ibonus turned away as if suddenly bored of this new primate and now remained content with simply grazing on the fields all day. He probably had no interest in serving as a hero's companion unless I could feed him some very delicious grass or bring him a sexy female member of his odd species. Still, the stupid idea in my head seemed cool enough for me to try out. I snuck just enough to the left to avoid the creature's powerful hind legs and got closer and closer.

"Just try it!" I declared as I jumped onto Ibonus' back and grabbed his neck. The creature was agitated and buckled back

and forth, and I felt his rough hide scrape at my cheeks as I
clung with all my grip strength. "Calm down, boy!" I tried to
maintain my grip, but bulging muscles and skin continued to
slip away from my fingers as my entire body jilted. If my arms
weren't enough, what was the trick?

*Mongol warriors trained enough to fire arrow after arrow on
horseback, so . . . my legs!*

I channeled all my energy into my leg muscles, trying to
get my Diamorph transformation to augment my muscles just
enough, just like it had done in the fight against the crocodiles
and against Bethany. As my arms came loose, I felt my entire
upper body toss around like a ragdoll, but miraculously, my
inner thighs kept their grip as my muscles strained against
Ibonus' sides. "Aagghhaahah . . . " I saw the clouds as my
head swung wildly in the chaotic ride, and then the grass, and
then the clouds again, and then . . .

Thonk!

One leg suddenly came loose as I felt a face full of bark, and
I spun in the air at least twice before collapsing onto the soft
grass. Ibonus had been smart enough to run toward the nearest tree and smash me against a low-hanging branch. When I
struggled to my feet and cleared the dizzy lines from my vision, I could see that Ibonus was galloping far off into the distance.

"You almost did it!" Sutoff declared as he jogged up to me.
"If you manage to make such a powerful beast your mount,
you'll end up being fit to lead our tribe after all." I had definitely done some kind of Diamorph transformation in my
legs, for when I stepped forward, I found it hard to walk. My
muscles were still struggling to shrink and untwist themselves, apparently.

"Thanks for the . . . optimism, but I'm going to lie down,
really," I started. "Maybe all I need is an ocarina and learn
what music Ibonus likes, huh?" Of course, Sutoff didn't quite
get the reference. People really took cars and even buses and

trains for granted, for I couldn't imagine how so many generations of men had fed, watered, and maintained horses, camels, and donkeys. And, best of all, the hero had to step up to the challenge and deal with the most stubborn creature of all when it came to his ride.

Sutoff helped me a little with my limping as I made my way back toward Oljatu's camp. The khan of the tribe seemed more impressed than disappointed at my exploits, and he chuckled when I told him that I discovered I had to focus on leg strength.

"The modern generation with its chairs everywhere," Oljatu said. "Not even the strength to squat like a child." My distant ancestor put a hand on my shoulder, looking at me with confident expectations. "You want to just go out and spar, but you'll have to develop leg strength, as well, if you want to ride an animal across these wild plains. We'll spend the rest of this afternoon and evening mostly on stance training."

Latis was apparently keeping up with my exploits and seemed to be in a good mood despite still recovering from his injuries. "So that's another stroke of good luck for you on your journey, Abyss," he said with a smile. "First, you run into your distant ancestors, and next, you find an unstoppable mount to conquer."

"Should we really be hanging out with Oljatu's tribe for so long, though?" I stepped over and asked him. "I know that I need to keep on training, but if it prevents us from getting to the next oil spring and restoring the diamond blade, won't that be a problem?"

"Beats me." Latis shrugged. "I've never been the type to look for clues and give hints to heroes I'm told to assist, as most quests aren't this complicated."

I turned back toward Oljatu and decided to begin the training. I tried my best not to overthink things and fought my lazy inclinations. The stance training was as boring as it sounded, but at the same time, it didn't make things any less painful. It only took a few minutes for my inner thighs to begin shaking and burning, and the tribesmen would repeatedly force me to a stable position. Getting blown out in a basketball game or sitting through a dull class hadn't been so troublesome, had it?

"I wonder how Sonny and Simon are doing," I muttered to myself as I also switched from stance to stance and stretched my hips and arms. Sonny did say that developing leg muscles was needed for movement in boxing and martial arts and had found that I was underdeveloped in that area. Still, the long and sweating persistence hunt was preferable to these low stances. Oljatu and his men would bark and threaten me if I ever lost balance or posture, and my legs began to shake and grow numb. I envied both large and small cats terribly for having such natural strength and speed and being able to sleep most of the day away.

"Stomp." Oljatu demonstrated to me as he stood across in the *horse* stance, lifting his feet just an inch or two and making a powerful stomp on the dirt ground. I suppose it was reasonable given how bumpy things could get riding on horseback and emulated Oljatu's movement. My feet barely made any noise as they sunk, but I could still feel the shock coursing through my lower body. As my form and concentration broke, the tribesmen began to exclaim further skepticism regarding my abilities.

"Are you sure that we should have bothered to save him and feed him?" one of the men asked. "He's so weak . . ."

"He will demonstrate his worth soon enough," Oljatu said. "No matter how sheltered his environment was, he's young enough to grow into the role of a hero."

I stepped back into my horse stance and let the minutes begin to stretch into hours. Even if this world didn't have a convenient villain to defeat, I remembered how Justin looked down upon me at the Western Sanctuary, and how Grigory and the Pharaoh just saw me as a tool. At the very least, I wanted to become strong enough to determine my own destiny. But how many men throughout the eras had marched into battle wanting to bring glory to their family and motherland, only to be mowed down in a few minutes by a storm of arrows or cannon fire?

I could hardly walk at the end of the day as I ate dinner, and with sore muscles and a weary mind, I began to drift off toward sleep.

While I saw random flashes and memories, I wasn't greeted to another warm welcome of the *friendly* Diana with my hidden power. Instead, I woke up to hear the sound of screams and panicking as the morning sun streamed into my eyes.

"She's been kidnapped!" I heard Sutoff declare. My legs were still sore from yesterday's training, and my stomach still growled, but I forced myself to peer out of the tent.

"That should be impossible! What a slight has befallen the Jalair tribe!"

Latis seemed to be up and ready for action after spending half of yesterday recovering from his injuries. Although his broken arm was in a sling, he rode on a brown pony and scouted the area before approaching me. "Looks like another everyday occurrence for the tribes of the grasslands," Latis commented. "Rutyll, the most beautiful girl of this tribe, has been kidnapped by their rivals. And we're going to go and bring her back."

Oljatu saw that I'd awoken and handed me a quick breakfast of preserved meat and cheese. "Now's your chance to prove your worth, young Abyss." My legs were really screaming at me to at least take the morning off, but when

Oljatu acknowledged me, more and more of the tribesmen's eyes turned in my direction.

"I'll have to share a horse . . ."

Whiiieeenenene! A half-neighing, half-bleating sound came from a familiar large, horned animal as it strolled through the rows of tents. Ibonus had paid me a visit for some reason and looked at me with curious eyes. He hadn't seemed to acquire the ability to speak yet, and I still found it extremely risky to get on his back. But I remembered how thick this creature's hide supposedly was and also considered the worst-case scenario where my horse would be shot, and I would be flung across the ground like a ragdoll.

"I'm not that heavy, so don't panic." I stepped up to Ibonus and rubbed his cheek a little before I turned toward his side. I was still trying to quickly force the food Oljatu had given me down my throat when he made an official announcement as chieftain.

"Today will be a glorious day!" Oljatu announced. "Now that the horned beast has even volunteered to serve under our new successor, Abyss, we shall be able to march across the Eastern plains and continue our path toward glory, conquest, and victory! They think they can take our lovely Rutyll and get away with it, but we will slaughter all of their men and enslave their women and children!" It was as barbaric and merciless as any tribal warrior, and I gulped anxiously, worried whether or not I would be able to change this culture at all. If this was a video game, it felt like I was being dragged into a side-quest and making all the wrong decisions.

The one saving grace I had was the fact that Ibonus allowed me to ride on his back. However, with that came testing my sore and weak legs with every gallop, and for some reason, Oljatu allowed me to lead the charge on my mount. He'd only given me a short sword after I'd explained that I still had no experience with arrows or slings. In the end, I would probably have to rely on Ibonus to do most of the dirty work and then hope my sore legs would allow me to stand up against whatever opponents I had to fight on foot.

"The scouts have seen us," Oljatu said as he rode up onto my side. "If they flee, we will mow them down. If they fight, we have good odds. Even if we're outnumbered four to one, I can take out six or seven men before my horse even suffers damage, and you carry our trump card with the horned monster you tamed."

It appeared that the opposing tribe had decided to fight us after all, and were similarly adept with using bows and arrows on horseback. The first few arrows volleyed back and forth as I tried to stay protected behind Ibonus' thick skull and neck, but Oljatu was quickly displaying his superior skills. He rarely had to shoot the much larger horse, and rider after rider began falling with shafts sprouting from their heads and chests. It would have been a lot more gruesome if these men hadn't been reincarnations from the dead, as thankfully their bodies began to dissolve into golden mist, similar to my previous foes.

Ibonus quickly stepped into the fray and displayed his monstrous speed and strength. As his rider, I was forced along a wild ride. Apparently, he most preferred to jump high enough to knock riders off their horses, as if his main intent was to set his distant relatives free. By a miracle, none of the arrows hit me, and the ones that found Ibonus' back, side, and front were easily stopped by his thick hide and quickly fell off within a couple of seconds.

"The rider! Just knock the rider off!" Some of the opposing tribesmen began to yell. I quickly noticed that Ibonus had dragged me way into the territory of the enemy tribe and that I was now cut off from the rest of the Jalair tribe. Ibonus thrust and smashed with his skull and horns, but ultimately, there were too many opposing tribesmen. I was able to dodge a few lucky spear thrusts and sword strikes before I began to lose my balance. My mount wobbled to the side just enough, and my sore legs gave out from under me. I spun into the air for a couple of seconds before collapsing onto the ground. When I managed to open my eyes and look up, I felt the cold metal of a blade kiss my throat.

"Are you sure we can just kill him? He might have the key to taming those horned monstrosities." The enemy tribesmen began to debate amongst each other.

"What's more, he doesn't seem to be resurrected. Maybe he's the boy that pulled out the diamond blade and allowed us to reform," another tribesman suggested.

"He's a descendant of the Jalair tribe, no matter how far removed, isn't he?" The man pressing the sword against my throat asked. "Even if it meant canceling our own existence, I won't allow their kind to succeed."

The only thing I could do was bluff. "If you kill me, you'll never be able to meet the God of Fire. I might be a descendant of whatever tribe, but my blood lineage doesn't determine my destiny. I'll swear allegiance to whatever tribe, whatever kingdom proves itself worthy and . . . " The blade pressed further into my throat, but luckily, there was still enough time for plan B. If I could make a coiled spring out of my leg and chuck Diana way up into the air with augmented arm muscles, simple hardening should be possible.

I pushed my neck upward toward the blade, and the Diamorph transformation had hardened the front of my neck just enough. The man loosened his grip on his blade in surprise, and I went for the fastest and easiest move. I bit two exposed fingers from the man's right hand, twisting my head to the left as I chomped down with all my might. I didn't have time to cringe in disgust as I quickly picked up the abandoned blade, slashing one of the tribesmen that had surrounded me as I stumbled forwards.

"Ibonus!" I called, and to my surprise, the horse-ibex hybrid began galloping back toward me.

Ibonus smashed his head against the three pursuers behind me, giving me some breathing room as I spit out the dissipating remnants of the two fingers I'd bitten off. I rubbed my neck as well, finding that it was slowly reverting to weak human flesh.

"Thanks a lot, buddy," I said to Ibonus as I clambered onto his back. The enemy tribe had a hard time surrounding me once again. For now, Oljatu and Latis had made it into the enemy tents and were laying waste and havoc with fury and barbaric glee. Latis was especially impressive with only one arm. He found his mark with throwing knives while he bobbed and weaved away from swords and spears on horseback.

"Young Abyss has cleared the defenses and led the charge!" Oljatu announced as he continued to empty his quiver of arrows. The cavalry that attempted to thrust at him with spears and swords were easily outmaneuvered by his nimble riding.

However, it seemed like Ibonus' main interest hadn't been mere chaos. The horned beast led me toward the outpost where the opposing tribe had tied up their horses, yak, and sheep, and I saw another odd member of Ibonus' family, this one with gray spots on his fur and looking dejected. The second horse-ibex hybrid was tied up to a series of heavy boulders with reinforced ropes.

"Poor guy," I muttered. Ibonus neighed in concern once more as he shook about and made his intents clear without having to speak a single word. I dismounted from my horned companion as I withdrew the short sword Oljatu had given me. "He'll go free," I said to Ibonus. "It's the least I could do in exchange for all your help." The ropes were tough and difficult to cut with the short sword, and without the jagged edge of a saw, I hacked at the ropes multiple times until they split into breakable strings. The trapped ibex-horse whinnied in delight as it galloped off into the distance.

"So that's what he was after, huh?" I heard Latis comment as he rode toward me on his brown pony. "We got Rutyll and some more goods to boot, although many of the survivors of the enemy tribe managed to escape. You sort of let your mount carry you hard in battle, although I guess things will improve with time."

"And my legs are going to be even more sore," I said as I rubbed Ibonus on the cheeks. "I think we've had our daily share of deadly action sequences." Even now, I was too hopeful that my adventure wasn't intent on pushing me toward the brink of exhaustion.

"The best spoils of today's raid shall go to the one that enabled our victory, our new successor, Abyss!" Oljatu declared as he stood in the center of the Jalair tribe. I was expecting fancy equipment, armor, or even magical runes, but instead, Oljatu brought out a rather pretty girl that couldn't be much older than me. "Rutyll will be available for another successful conquest, but it has always been the Jalair tradition to first make the conquered wives and slaves before arranging marriages for those born into our tribe."

"I . . . " I knew I needed to choose my words carefully, but I was beginning to get fed up with the amorality of my ancestors' lifestyles. "We got Rutyll back, and we killed or injured most of the enemy tribe. Should we really be so eager to make those we conquered slaves?"

Oljatu once again looked at me with disbelief and disappointment. "We are a small tribe," he decided. "With little technology on top of it. No one in their right mind would waste a fertile womb attached to a beautiful and healthy girl." The newly acquired slave didn't seem to express hope upon

hearing my objection—like Rutyll, she had long been prepared for the brutality of life on the grasslands.

I was flabbergasted. Even if I didn't have Diana in my
mind, I couldn't just tolerate taking a girl as a slave. "I'll re-
lease her and see if she can adjust to modern civilization."
Oljatu seemed prepared to laugh, but he knew that I wasn't
joking regarding such a suggestion.

The chieftain shook his head. "If you won't take her as a
slave, I will." My legs were still sore from yesterday's training
and the wild ride on Ibonus a few hours ago. I didn't stand a
chance in battle if I was fully rested, let alone in this condition.

"Is this how life should be, Oljatu?" I pressed. "Every man
a living weapon and every woman a womb? Even though you
know that with science, technology, and cultural progress,
humans can live more fulfilled lives?"

"Don't get cocky just because you managed to ride the
horned beast." Oljatu stepped forward. "Your generation is
too soft, pathetically sheltered. While dreaming of saving
princesses from monsters, you work long hours in little cubicles to buy pointless luxuries and products. Modern man only
works to please the crowd, so far removed from the beauty
and cruelty of nature. The men of your time do little other
than feed their bellies and let a screen with images dictate
where they come and go. You have long forgotten what true
power is."

"If I just wanted power, I could be a lion or a hippo." I tried
to sound as confident as possible. "Humans can be something
more—"

"Abyss, step down," Latis interjected. I shrugged the
spiky-haired boy off, and Oljatu actually grinned at me.

"Even if misguided, I like your fight, my distant descendant. We shall duel over what happens to Moka, the captured
slave!" None of the other tribesmen seemed to have objec-
tions. "Have a small snack, but be ready within ten minutes."

113

"Abyss, what are you thinking?" Latis asked after Oljatu turned away to prepare for the duel. "Trying to be a hero and saving random slaves you don't even know won't get you further on your actual mission. You know, the quest to return the diamond blade and all! This really isn't a video game where you can just put the main storyline on hold. Neither is it a children's book where everything will work out in the end."

I looked away. "You can call me soft-hearted for that. Any tips specifically for fighting Oljatu?"

"You're a goner," Latis said. "I trained you as hard as possible, and you put good effort with stance training, but there's a limit to how much you can crutch on your Diamorph transformations."

I snacked on some more preserved meats and cheeses, but I knew that my body needed at least another full night of sleep to fully recover. My agility and mobility would probably be halved on my sore legs, and even if I could reinforce my arms and fists, my punches would probably break their form mid-strike. I turned again at Moka, who was being watched over by the other tribesmen.

"I'll find some way for you," I said, unsure if she could understand or speak English. "I know that you just reincarnated into the modern day, but there are plenty of good people outside your tribe."

Moka had no interest in my suggestion. "You're the stupidest boy I've ever seen," she said, and I forced myself to grin.

The Jalair tribe wasn't too skilled musically, but in preparation for an official duel, around six men alternated between drumbeats, woodwind instruments, and simple singing. Oljatu removed his light armor strapped underneath, as apparently, it would be a simple fistfight. My stomach churned as I remembered how poorly my matches against Simon and Grigory had been. Even if Oljatu wasn't as tall as them, he still had the definite height, weight, and experience advantage.

"For the sake of the lovely newly conquered slave Moka, our great chieftain Oljatu and the young newcomer in our tribe, Abyss, face off in fisticuffs!" Some of the younger members of the tribe gazed at us curiously, but no one was rooting for me to pull off the upset. "The duel begins in three . . . two . . . one . . ."

My legs were already beginning to ache as I strafed about and tried to find an opening. Oljatu grew impatient, and so he pressed the offense. If I could transform any part of my body, I just needed my arms. Maybe provide some body armor for my abdomen, the next biggest target . . .

I was definitely moving too slowly to bob and weave between the punches, so I covered my face with my arms and left my gut and abdomen exposed.

Thud.

I stumbled backward as Oljatu's punch connected with my stomach. I gasped for air, but I could still stand up on my sore legs. While I peered between my forearms, I could see my distant ancestor form an amused smile.

"You're getting better at your special power," he observed. "Now, if only you had the proper attitude to match it!"

Oljatu didn't seem to mind damaging his forearms or knuckles and continued to pummel at my partially reinforced abdomen. I could feel small bits of my breakfast and lunch come back up through my throat and knew that I had to counterattack eventually. I made a quick jab with my left, just enough to throw Oljatu off and readjust myself. Now just to follow it with a strong right . . .

My sore legs made everything slow and awkward. Oljatu grabbed me by the arm and tossed me up in the air, just as Simon had done. It didn't matter that I'd finally awakened the powers I'd gotten from the Witch or if he couldn't teleport at will. I was still a boy way over his head on this journey, trying to do things that would only work in fiction. My body crashed against the hard dirt clearing, and as I bounced up in mid-air, only one thought came to my mind.

Run.

At this level, I couldn't even get Oljatu to break a sweat. I'd have to put all of my Diamorph transformation into my legs now as I tumbled over. I looked at Moka and found that her hands were tied behind her back, but she wasn't chained or behind bars as another tribesman held her hostage. Oljatu might be really disappointed in me, and I would cause further trouble for Latis later on—but I didn't even care about the hero's quest anymore, and I doubted that I would ever understand the true purpose of the universe if I met the God of Fire. All I wanted to do was save Moka, and I believed that it would make the world better, just by a little.

I could feel the muscles in my legs twisting and readjusting, but this time, it occurred much faster than it had in the swamp with the coiled spring. If I'd been wearing pants instead of shorts, they would have been easily ripped in the process, for my bottom half now began to look more like an ostrich's proportions. I bolted forward with my new form and pretended to attack Oljatu. He bought it, and so did the rest of the audience, bewildered by my sudden transformation.

Plud!

I smashed Moka's retainer with one of my ostrich legs and slung the girl over my shoulder, unsure of where exactly I would flee to. Diana hadn't even properly taught me how to make a fire, and I doubt I could find a sanctuary for Witches and heroes that would accept Moka. Even if the Jalair tribe could chase me on horseback, I easily zigzagged to disguise my tracks in the tall grass. I ran for at least several minutes while Moka just dangled helplessly, and before I could stop and think, a gang of wild cheetahs had decided that Moka and I would make tasty afternoon snacks.

"Ibonus!" I yelled, but the horned hybrid didn't seem interested in my problems any longer. I knew that I couldn't outrun these cheetahs, especially while carrying additional weight on my shoulders. Could I put Moka down and possibly fight them? That also seemed equally ridiculous. The cheetahs were getting closer and closer and would be upon us in less than half a minute.

"Cats and water," I mumbled to myself as I saw that the small cliff in front of us overlooked a large, rushing river. "Moka, hold your breath!" I declared as I jumped off the cliff and plunged straight into the raging waters.

CHAPTER FIVE

"Uohhhkoffggh, oyuhgahha!" I spit out a mouthful of water as I struggled to surface for air with Moka still slung over my back. I would let the river continue to carry me far away from the Jalair tribe while I paddled toward the shore. "All right, looks like we'll . . . oh good grief!"

The good thing about landing in the river was that it automatically carried the two of us downstream, while the bad thing was that we weren't alone here — a school of hungry piranha had also somehow found their way into this ecosystem, and like the cheetahs, considered us a convenient source of protein.

"Hang in there, Moka!" I yelled as I desperately tried to stay afloat while I ripped off the piranhas that were gnawing at my arms.

It was no use — there were too many of them, and each of them was stripping away bits of flesh no larger than a fingernail. Death by the cheetahs would be much faster and less painful, but . . . *like hell, I was going to die here!* Even if it meant forcing another Diamorph transformation and putting my whole body through hellish aching, I would survive. The oceans covered over two-thirds of the planet, and there were endless branches of evolution when it came to aquatic beings. If I could somehow manage ostrich legs, why not a dolphin?

I still had to stay near the surface to ensure that Moka was breathing, and I still wanted to keep my arms, obviously. But if I just transformed my legs yet again . . . my bones cracked and split as the muscles again twisted. I could still feel each leg separately, but they were weaved together by new folds of skin, and within a few seconds, I'd become somewhat of a merman. Unfortunately, that by itself wasn't enough to discourage the piranhas from feasting on me. I needed more transformation. Teeth, a longer snout, and maybe a thick, tough layer of blubber . . .

All's fair in the game of food. You can eat me, but I can also eat you.

Moka somehow managed to cling onto me as I used my arms to grab the piranhas nearby and redirect them toward my new dolphin-like jawbones. I'd never been fond of sushi, but the raw piranha definitely surpassed the beetle larvae and raw eggs in taste, if not in nutrients. The simple stories of heroes wielding swords and shields had always been cool enough for me, but now I was beginning to appreciate the heroes and superpowers of the natural world.

Even if I only had a slice of the branches of the endless tree of life, I took this moment to relish munching down piranha after piranha and creating a bloody mess. My throat had evolved just enough so that the bones didn't choke me, but the sharp edges still scraped at my esophagus as they made their way down.

Eventually, the piranhas had decided that I was more trouble than I was worth. It was a good thing because my new bottom half was beginning to ache on top of my leg soreness. Even though I'd just eaten, I couldn't just instantly convert the protein into energy in my stomach. My mind and brain were still human, especially, and I needed to rest somewhere, somehow. I swam toward the edge of the river as my lower half began to revert to two-legged, human form.

I didn't know how many miles the river had taken us, but it had become weak and narrow enough as it became more of a creek within the lush forests. It might be likely that a hungry bear or a pack of wolves would assault me in my sleep, but my eyelids were growing heavy as I clambered back onto solid ground.

When I put Moka down, I realized that she was bleeding everywhere from the piranha bites. I stumbled toward the forest to find anything that could save her, but my legs gave out from under me as I slumped to my knees. Tears began to form in the corners of my eyes.

I was just a stupid fool who thought that he could save everybody. Moka had been prepared for a life as a slave, and she would have lived decently long even amongst the warring tribes. And what had I done? I'd taken her to become prey for cheetahs, and then piranha food, and then . . . probably food for scavengers and then decomposers in the ruthless cycle of life and death. Even if I survived, what would happen then?

Would I become a simpleton only in the adventure to fight like Latis was, or a cynical wanderer like Diana? Or would my failure here proceed to haunt me forever?

"Aaaaaarrrrgh . . . " I groaned as I collapsed onto the nearby creek edge. In my last bouts of consciousness, I crossed my fingers and hoped that someone out there would save us.

When I awoke, I was far deeper into the mysterious forest, but there were no signs of human civilization. Moka was also completely gone, and as I sat up, I realized that my legs and knees still buckled with pain. When I attempted to stand up, I heard soft, various cracking noises as if I had far too many extra bones and muscles near my thighs. I stumbled backward and fell once more, grumbling under my breath. I also noticed that I was fatigued and dizzy, dehydrated, as well as craving more food. It wouldn't surprise me if I'd been out for over twelve hours.

"Anyone there?" I asked. There was a short silence for a while, and then, as if to answer, a beautiful, ripe apple fell down from the tree branches and landed in front of me. As I picked up the fruit and inspected it, I heard the rumble of more objects in the canopy above. One after another, fruits of all shapes, sizes, and colors fell from above and littered the ground with a bounty that markets could only dream of. That's right, it had to be a dream, an illusion, or a dirty trick being played on me . . .

Grrreerrrreerrwwllwl!

My stomach was groaning like a cornered animal, and I knew I couldn't argue with it. I took a clean bite of the apple and realized that I hadn't had fresh fruit in over a week — I didn't eat cereal or candies for that matter, either, and the natural sugars were a reminder of the wonders of the human tongue. I had never filled up on fruit before and knew that I would have to eat a lot compared to slices of meat or grains. But as long as my mobility was limited to crawling forwards and backward on my injured legs, I needed whatever fuel I could find to retool my body.

"Delicious, isn't it?" A woman's voice called out. I looked around, but I saw no one as I munched ravenously on a grapefruit.

"Um," I started in between bites. "Are you a Witch that's able to turn invisible?"

"I'm something far greater," the voice answered. "To think that the legendary Witch contracted with a hero that could similarly appreciate the wonders of life — perhaps it really is destiny."

I scratched my head and took a wild guess. "You're the tree that dropped all of these fresh fruits for me? If you are, thanks for letting me rest, but what about Moka?"

"She'll survive for now, but everything will be questionable when you restore the diamond blade and confront the God of Fire. I once concerned myself merely with the troubles of the human species, just like you're doing now, young Abyss."

I chewed through the bitter pulp of the fruit, crawled over to some mangoes, and awkwardly tried to peel away the skin.

"I could produce more than fruit with my ability to synthesize chemicals, and once saved many with medicines and drugs that could deeply mutate an organism's DNA. But once I discovered the full potential of my power, human beings simply seemed less and less significant."

"But . . . " I wondered. "Are you a fellow Witch at all? Or a different species that human beings had never stumbled on before?"

"I started as a Witch but ended up as something far greater. The God of Fire granted us magic so that we attempted to bring salvation to mankind, but I asked, *why stop there*? What about the millions, billions of different animals that starve daily, that get eaten alive due to cruel fate? What about the trillions of extinct organisms who weren't able to leave behind descendants and continue their legacy?"

I squeezed the flavor out of my mango and wondered if this mysterious nature goddess was asking a trick question. "But if we were to stay in a world of zero suffering, zero injustice regarding all species, we wouldn't be able to advance past unicellular life, creatures that don't quite feel pain," I started. I tried to recall what I'd learned in my science classes. "Once we developed past unicellular life, almost everything began to evolve eyes and a brain, and pain . . . the capacity to suffer to increase odds of survival. And as it stands, I think it'd take an awful lot of magic to provide enough food if everything became herbivorous. The only thing stopping deer and the like from turning the fields into rough desert are the wolves . . ."

"And yet you went through all that effort to save Moka, a girl that you hardly knew. And someone that shouldn't even have been here. You didn't abandon her to be a breeding slave, like unfortunate ducks and dolphins often become, and you didn't let her become food for the cheetahs and piranhas."

I sighed and tried to gather my thoughts as I began peeling another mango. "I was a foolish kid trying to play hero then. Maybe . . . maybe Oljatu is right and that all we're doing right now is entertaining ourselves."

"It will be possible if you try," the nature goddess said. "The world can know happiness and intelligence in a world without aggression and carnivores. You will become the key to my end goal, for that, I caught a glimpse of your future."

I shook my head.

Even if this nature goddess was friendly enough to give me fruit, and even if her goals weren't as brutal as the Pharaoh's or Oljatu's, I still found it too absurd. "It sucked to usually be the last pick on the basketball courts, and it sucked to be a nerdy kid that was bullied, but I'm not sure I'd prefer a world with no aggression . . . and then it's back in a circle."

I picked up a pear and crunched on it after finishing my second mango. "That in the first place, aggression and competition are only evolved mechanisms when brains become complex enough. Then why not go back to mere unicellular life? Why give me fruit? Why have life in the first place, and why not merely be satisfied with earth as another small, terrestrial planet orbiting an average solar system?"

"It's obviously nothing to be reasoned about," the nature goddess replied. "When you traversed the paths of evolution twice in your escape . . . first borrowing from the ostrich, then from the dolphins, you witnessed sheer beauty that doesn't deserve its inevitable suffering and extinction. That's enough reason to assist me in my quest to let nature bloom and flourish, is it not?"

"But nature still has to exist in the realm of the grander scale of physics," I said. "The sun will become too large, too hot for most lifeforms. Unless there's a next life, all humans can do, from scientists to philosophers to artists, is appreciate and analyze the wonders of the natural world. Even if I pulled some magical stunts here and there, I don't want to shape-shift into every species, present and future, and become their own personal Jesus."

The nature goddess didn't make an objection, but apparently, she still felt like I was shackling myself to rationality. I would have to ingest a large amount of hallucinogens before agreeing that nature was something that could be tied to the deep cosmos of the universe. As I reached for a bundle of grapes, I saw a cute gray cat walk up to me slowly with the remains of a rodent in its mouth. I scratched my head for a while and wondered how bizarre my life could get.

"Can you also talk?" I asked the cat, but the feline didn't even meow. "Maybe I'll never be as strong as a tiger or a lion, or as fast as a cheetah, but I would at least be able to jump and move like you guys can. It's probably impossible on two limbs, but without a weapon and with my size disadvantage, it's the only way I'll be able to stop taking losses when I fight grown men." Now that my legs had recovered a little, I still felt my abs and sides ache from the hard pummeling that Oljatu had given me. I honestly wished that I had just been given a cool power like Simon had instead of having to painfully shift my body structure whenever I borrowed the abilities of other animals.

"Meow," the cat asserted as it finished the remains of its prey. It started walking back and forth, as if trying to demonstrate something.

"Is this all I have for reference?" I asked the nature goddess and had no response. "Big or small, domestic or wild, you felines sure are lucky." I saw as I knelt down to observe the cat's movements. "You get to sleep and laze around for most of the day while humans are stuck hunched over in class or forced into little cubicles at work." I decided to shadow the cat's movements, although on two legs rather than four. It was like I was doing a defense drill for basketball again.

And then the cat picked up the speed and showed me what it was truly capable of. Within a small span of two meters or so, the cat sprinted as fast as any Olympic runner could, but it managed to switch its direction and almost made a pure one-eighty turn in less than half a second and darted back. This was the acceleration, the change of direction that would make any superstar NBA guard jealous, as the cat bounced back and forth a few times before it came to a slow halt and sat down on its paws. I sighed as I tried to mimic the motion.

It had to be the fact that I was a biped and the fact that I lacked a tail. If cats could laugh, I'm sure I would be ridiculed for my clumsiness as I tried to mimic the cat's sudden directional changes. I kept at it for a good hour or so before I exhausted myself once more and continued to feast on the abundant fruit. Everything really was frustrating. A real-life adventure was never as convenient as comics and video games when it came to learning new techniques or acquiring new equipment.

"I wonder if Latis or Inder will come and find me," I mumbled to myself. Now I really missed Diana, even if she still found me annoying. "How hard does everything have to be anyways? Just give me what every hero has in fantasy novels. A male friend and a supportive female, and let me just run about, shout, and scream like an idiot."

Of course, the weird nature goddess and the gray cat couldn't respond to my requests. All I could do was mimic the movements of the gray cat as I shifted back and forth. My toes began to curve significantly. The nails turned into claws, and the soles of my feet became more like pads — my sandals had broken ever since the ostrich transformation, so I'd been going barefoot. While I still wasn't close to the speed of the cat, I saw significant improvement as the hours began to pass, although the pain in my ankles, knees, and toes was yet another fresh stimulation that I could go without. Within a few more weeks, I would probably break and bend every muscle in my body, trying to pull off these Diamorph transformations.

Thok. Thok.

Two arrow shafts sprouted from the ground beside me, and again, I falsely raised my hopes. When I turned toward the direction of the projectiles, I saw a lightly armored man wave to me and immediately readied for combat.

"We have kept tabs on you from a distance, young Abyss," the armored man said. He was definitely wearing the same outfit as the Pharaoh's regiment that Grigory had commanded. "You've made progress and displayed your strongest motivation to unlock your full potential."

I sighed. "Tell Grigory that I'm not interested in joining his plan to purge the world."

"If you don't come, Diana will be repeatedly tortured."

I stormed up to the man and tried to remind myself that he was just the messenger.

"Within less than an hour, you managed two significant metamorphoses with your power and bit down the pain and internal damage it caused you. Your soft spot is saving girls in danger, isn't it?"

I remembered how Grigory had been amused rather than disturbed when I ripped off his left arm during my first Diamorph transformation. If I agreed to his terms, I would just be playing into his hands, but I really didn't want to let Diana suffer because of my indecision. "Take me to him, and we can have a face-to-face talk. And then another fist-to-fist showdown."

The man nodded as he turned and gestured for me to follow him. I turned back at the mysterious nature goddess one more time and found that she had no commentary to add to it. "What about you?" I asked the armored figure. "I know that you were probably brainwashed from an early age into serving the Pharaoh, be it in combat or in ceremony, but haven't you thought that you could use your new life to live for yourself this time?"

"It's true that the modern world offers a large amount of luxuries," the man answered. "But you have also not yet seen how truly great our Pharaoh is when it comes to the plans for advancing humanity."

I fell into silence and wanted to save my energy and my best arguments for when I met Grigory face-to-face again. I also wondered if Diana would be frustrated at my eagerness to save her just like it had been in the fight against Bethany. I didn't want to fall into another bizarre oil field and be repeatedly eaten alive by dozens of different species, and I wondered if things would be any worse this time.

The camp that Grigory had settled down in was a rather simple clearing filled with tents, much like the Jalair tribe and other nomads had set up.

"He's arrived, Diana." Grigory turned toward my mentor, who had been tied up to a stake with an assortment of knives, arrowheads, and poisonous substances in containers beside her. Grigory looked amused at my determined expression, confident that he'd chosen the right plan. "You've gotten stronger, but you still remain so immature mentally."

"Why drag her into this in the first place?" I asked. "She's already served the Pharaoh for years in her original lifetime, and he can move on . . ."

"For the very reason that her fate is entangled with yours, young Abyss," Grigory said. "Your distant ancestor Oljatu wanted you to be a mere conqueror of tribes, which is a fraction of your potential destiny. And yet you still cling to such dastardly ideals of romance. To waste away life for the mere sake of the female is a peacock's job, not something befitting man."

"I'm not one of your video game princesses." Diana turned

to me. "Focus on your mission and restore the diamond blade, Abyss." That was Diana, all right, always headstrong and stubborn, even if she was about to be tortured.

I wanted to simply jump up and punch Grigory in the face, but I remembered how poorly things had gone with Oljatu just a couple of days ago. "And what would you have me do as another of the Pharaoh's servants?" I asked him.

"The world has an overabundance of mindless hedonism," Grigory said as he revealed his left arm, which had previously been covered in a sleeve. It looked even worse than my right arm had gotten when I'd pulled off the initial Diamorph transformation, as it bulged with purple and green nerves between the awkwardly twisted muscles. "The desire you have to save Diana, or any other human in danger, is something you'll have to outgrow. However noble that instinct may seem, it is no different than the fox that raids and kills to feed her kits or even the ants and bees that gladly work and die for their kind. Humankind has the potential to explore and understand the depths of the universe, but instead, they trap themselves worrying about little pleasures, meaningless lives."

Grigory now turned to Diana and gestured to his men to ready the torture devices. "Diana herself knows how fleeting your existence is, having lived a full existence for over four millennia."

"Gryash . . . Grigory's right," Diana began. She bit down the pain as one of the poison spikes slowly wedged into her left arm. "I've had dozens of heroes rush in to try and save me, and that only ended in tragedy. Don't count yourself as special, Abyss . . ."

"Even if it's an endless cycle of violence, I don't care!" I stepped forward and confronted Grigory. "I'm only thirteen, and I might not know much more when I'm thirty or seventy, but only living for knowledge and efficiency is a mistake. I know that I screwed up a lot so far on my journey, and I know that I'll mess up until my last breath, but I'm not going to allow torture just for the sake of some greater good." I ran toward Diana, but Grigory moved in my path.

"Let's see how much you've grown, young hero." Apparently, he was satisfied with just hand-to-hand combat once more and was willing to risk losing another limb if I got a lucky transformation. Grigory immediately noticed my improved lateral movements, and his men cast a magical spell that surrounded the two of us in a boxing ring. "This time, things will be different," he declared. "Every time you fall to the ground, Diana will get another painful poison stake wedged into her body."

I gulped and remembered how beat up Moka's body had been after I carried her across the piranha-infested waters.

I hadn't been given enough time to learn from the gray cat, and I still had limited overall experience when it came to boxing. I tried to push to the left, fake right, and go left again, but no matter what, Grigory used his longer limbs to keep at a safe distance. He wasn't beating me mercilessly like in our first battle but instead threw quick jabs here and there. My face and body were sprinkled with quantity instead of quality. Eventually, after half a minute, both of my legs began to cramp up, and my toes could no longer handle the rapid acceleration and directional change.

"All you're doing is mimicking," Grigory observed. "But your transformative abilities are limited. You'll never be able to fully gain the traits of the animals that you seek to emulate." Why were things this way? My brain and spinal cord had to remain human at the very least. Even if it meant breaking my leg, I just wanted to smash Grigory's jaw with one decisive strike, but instead, my toes and feet began to wobble as I lost my footing.

Grigory knew that I was weak and dashed in with a swift

uppercut to my stomach. I tried my best to stay on two feet for Diana's sake, and I crouched as daggers scraped through my ankles. Grigory followed up with another gut punch, and I collapsed onto the hard dirt ground. I could see out of the corner of my eye that Diana was writhing in pain as another poisonous wedge carved into her arm. I cursed myself as I forced myself back to my feet.

I should be the one on the stake, and she should be in combat, shouldn't she?

But she was never even given the opportunity to become a hero, having simply been another one of the thousands of victims of the Pharaoh's conquest.

And that was when my weird sixth sense began to act up again. It was one of the reasons I could talk with the mysterious nature goddess, even if it was only for a brief moment. All consciousness, predator and prey, were connected in the chain of life. I'd wanted to take Diana's pain, even just a fraction of it, and . . . and what? Use it as a stimulant, another mindless piece of plot armor that could somehow ensure victory? Millions and billions of animals struggled throughout the history of Earth, as Grigory suggested. Empathy and grief were just evolutionary circuits, inevitable outcomes of being social animals. Even though I didn't visualize it, a spark seemed to fly from my head to Diana's, to all of the different creatures that I could possibly reach through space-time. But for now, all I could do was take her pain and feel the wedge and poison smash through my own arm.

"Excellent, Abyss," Grigory observed. "Your power might not be able to directly violate the laws of physics, like the teleporting hero, but you can bend the rules just enough, can't you?" My legs began to feel stable again, but the pain was still endless. It was as if where my skin touched the next atom, the world would be bent just enough to allow the proper movement. Even if I was too heavy and even if I was stuck with two limbs and no tail, I could learn to accelerate.

"Abyss!" Diana called out. She was still choking and gasping as the poison spread through her body. "You already bent reality enough when you fought against Bethany. Don't do it again!"

"And you've . . . " I turned to Diana. "You've spent far too long stuck wandering around for four thousand years. I know that I can find a happier ending for you somehow!" Grigory wanted to get a first-hand look at my new power. When he tossed a punch, I shuffled to the left, and with only two steps, I was almost behind him. I still couldn't push into a jump to reach his head or neck, but I could find a free hit on the rest of his body. Grigory turned as I socked him in the right abdomen. When he moved backward defensively, I continued my cat-like movements.

The five toes on each foot felt like they were twisting and being turned inside out whenever they hit the ground. But that split second of pain also distracted me from the pain that I was helping Diana relieve, and I tried my best to focus on my target. Grigory didn't know whether I was going to strike from the right or left, and he guarded the center of his chest.

I got too close too quickly, and even if he didn't know exactly what I would do, Grigory had enough general fighting experience. As I began to land on my front foot, he crouched down and performed a low-leg sweep, which sent me toppling off balance. I tried my best to land on my arms, but instead, I rolled across the ground to break my momentum. I immediately looked at Diana when I rolled over and saw that the poisonous spikes were now piercing through her right arm.

Maintain the connection. Remember why you're fighting.

Another burning, scraping sensation bombarded my right arm as I shared Diana's experience. Unfortunately, this time, I didn't feel renewed strength flowing through my limbs and knew that I had to defeat Grigory quickly.

"Why are you trying so hard?" Diana asked as she bit back her frustration. "You won't get anything from saving me."

"To continue to bumble about, generation after generation, like an ibex in mating season or a gorilla trying to assemble a harem, I see through your eyes that you're just a wild animal," Grigory said.

"Life is no movie, no comic book," I said thoughtlessly. "Maybe you're just another punk that stands in the way, like animals when they butt heads." When I went on the offensive this time, I was wary of leg sweeps and used my increased agility to weave back and forth as well as from side to side. No matter how experienced Grigory was, going for a big leg sweep or a front kick would always leave recoil that I could punish afterward.

"We've motivated him enough," Grigory decided, speaking to his men. "Send at least three more poisoned barbs into Diana, just to see how he reacts."

I gritted my teeth. If the fight would only end when I knocked Grigory out, I couldn't just bombard him with a slew of jabs. It would be too predictable if I tried to hit him with an augmented limb, so . . . I waited until another poisoned barb had pierced Diana's skin, this time in her left thigh. I wore an anguished expression on my face as I rushed toward Grigory with a powerful left kick.

Predictable, and I caught up in his two arms. Thankfully I was short and still could generate unnatural momentum with my right leg, kicking it backward to generate enough twisting flexibility as I concentrated my Diamorph transformation into my right fist.

"Too slow!" Grigory was shocked at my flexibility and sudden movement. I formed crystallized *diamond* knuckles that smashed Grigory through the jaw, and like in a horror movie, the flesh and bones on his face began to stream away. His teeth, lips, and cheeks were quickly turning into gas. And again, Grigory would have the last laugh as the remaining jaw muscles formed a toothy smile.

"I have served you, my Pharaoh . . ."

He lost his grip on my left leg a second after. As I landed on the ground, I heard powerful, chilling winds blow in from my right side, and the trees and leaves began to twist and turn, as if hit by a sudden mutation. Or perhaps they were communicating along the endless lines of evolution throughout both past and future as space and time began to bend. A thick fog started to blow in, and as I struggled back to my feet and tried to step toward Diana, I felt a very fine powder smash into my nose.

"There he is!" I heard a female's voice call out as the world began spinning around me. Was that Inder?

"He went ahead and abused the magic he was granted just to play hero again, huh?" This voice definitely came from Latis. "All I know is that we aren't going to follow your suggestions and scavenge for mushrooms."

"You've stumbled across the Titan's pit, too, haven't you?" Simon asked. "That's part of the power of the legendary Witch." I was floating in the midst of a quicksilver sea, and I saw that Simon was right beside me. "I want to have faith in your idealism, but the Witches have always differed when it came to how to save humanity."

"So am I caught up in a grand curse, a conspiracy whenever I use my power?" I asked. I saw a stream of memories pass by, and I soon learned that I was seeing myself from the outside. It was a bit embarrassing to have Simon here, but the tall redhead didn't pass judgment.

"Outside of the universe . . . outside space-time is the aether," Simon explained. "Although it seems like I can just choose where to teleport with my mind, I actually *exit* the boundaries of our universe and can swim through the aether with my physical body. If you've ever read *Flatland*, it's as simple as a three-dimensional object moving through a fixed two-dimensional plane, or the knight's unique ability to jump over other pieces in chess. Due to this power, I also receive odd dreams, but my power, for better or for worse, pales in comparison to yours."

"It's still awfully convenient for you," I commented. "Every time I use my power, I can feel my muscles and bones breaking as they borrow the structure of the animals I'm trying to emulate."

"But your potential exceeds mine, no matter how painful it gets," Simon said. "To put it simply, the Witches were caught up in the main argument as to what would constitute saving humanity. The two factions are supposedly equal in numbers, but one side believes that everything . . . memories, dreams, and nightmares must be preserved, and the other believes that evil and suffering must be simply eliminated. All signs from her recorded history suggests that the legendary Witch you contracted with believed in the former. That even if it meant having hundreds or thousands of ugly things for every beautiful moment, meaning must be made out of suffering."

"That's an awfully deep conversation. Perhaps it's better rephrased as questioning whether or not ignorance is bliss?" I asked.

"You still lived a fairly comfortable life." Simon's tone shifted a little. "It's best that no one gets their hands on your power. I'm willing to make compromises with the clerics that hunt down Witches and heroes in order to prevent you from damaging the boundaries between life and death, past and present, even further. And if you agree to it, you'll be returned to your everyday life unharmed."

I sighed. As I went through the last two years of middle school, I had slowly begun to realize that the world was more and more mundane. I'd desperately wished for something unusual and exciting to happen, but now that I was caught up in this mess of heroes and Witches, I realized that I wouldn't be lucky enough to stumble upon a happy ending. The quicksilver aether that showed my memories started to spiral together and project into the future, and it gave me a glimpse, a quick stream of shifting thoughts as to what would happen if I returned to the normal world.

Things had passed much faster than I'd anticipated. I'd discovered that seventh grade passed much faster than sixth grade and elementary school, but time would only continue to speed up. I saw myself growing through the typical teenage blues of a nerdy boy, hopelessly awkward around love interests, too distracted in class, and then more of the same in college. The time, thoughts, and feelings that usually were spent in a single day stretched out to a week and perhaps even a month as I entered my twenties. Work and chores would become the dominant routine as I paid the bills, and even fun things started to turn into gray tasks. And then . . . daydreamers never got their wish, and writers and artists ended up as tossed manuscripts or neglected corners of the internet. Friends quickly faded away as most of the people I met in school would stick to family or work—and speaking of family, I would be another disappointing child to overachieving parents. I would only bother putting enough effort into lower-level jobs like data entry and spend most of my earnings on rent. And while throwing away some tributes to entertainment, the time continued to accelerate as it passed by, until one day I would become another corpse in a box . . .

And it didn't matter what sort of religions monks and preachers peddled to me on the streets. A corpse was a corpse, and that would be the end of a normal life. No matter how complex the human brain was, our kind was no more deserving of salvation, of a greater purpose than ants and bees or wolves and dolphins. The best a living creature could do was pass on its genes and hoped that the next generation could be better. But in evolutionary terms, *better* only meant being more adept at surviving and reproducing. There was no room for heroes either in the animal kingdom or in crowded peaceful society full of distractions.

"I'm staying here, as bizarre and cruel as things get." I decided, still somewhat stuck in the path of future projection. "Maybe I'll end up in some tragic end with all my foolishness, but when survival is guaranteed, when maturity means that you celebrate less and grieve less, that's when the brain just turns itself off, and time gets meaninglessly faster."

"If that's so, then the next time we meet, things won't be pretty, Abyss," Simon said. As I continued drifting through the quicksilver aether, I started to feel like I was the one conjured by some struggling writer, and that mundane life where time passed all too quickly was the real *me* . . .

A pungent smell smashed into my nose as I twisted and turned in half-consciousness. Fire was dancing across my tongue and gums as I coughed madly and opened my eyes. I wanted to believe that the dream with Simon was just a dream, but it didn't quickly fade from memory. As my vision began to clear, Inder flashed me a cute smile as she gestured to her jar full of pickled and salted peppers. "I've still got the spices and all, so maybe we can try catching some easier food!"

My legs still felt twisted and shattered from the fight with Grigory, and as I looked around, I noticed that everything was shrouded in a thick fog. Objects more than three meters away dissolved into shadows peeking through the gray outlines, and Latis was the second to notice that I'd awoken, followed by Diana.

"Thanks to Abyss, space-time has been fractured enough so that we've now unleashed the mutagenic fog," the spiky-haired boy commented.

I wasn't in the mood to argue. I should consider myself lucky that I hadn't been abandoned out of frustration, but I really wished that Latis was more understanding. I turned over to Diana, who had wrapped her poisoned wounds in bandages and gauze. She tried to force a friendly smile when we caught gazes, but I knew that she still considered me a headstrong idiot.

"You've learned new techniques for sure," Diana said. "But your transformation still causes an immediate inconvenience, doesn't it?"

"Really, what were you thinking?" Latis asked. "Did you get full of yourself because you managed to ride Ibonus? Are we going to go through this quest while you try to save every girl you stumble across?"

"Is it really that bad?" I asked. "How bad could the fog be? We'll be fine as long as we stick together, right?"

"Everything changes in the fog," Inder said. "Very few things, from plants to animals we manage to kill are edible. The last time we got caught up in the fog, we were able to escape because the hero we were assisting could make many clones of himself and find the exit by marking the trees and the ground."

I struggled to my feet. My legs still wobbled from the pain. I noticed that the visible scars and tears in my skin had been frozen back in place to make quick clots, and icy stitches and splints forced some of the broken bone and cartilage back into their original position—or close enough, at least.

"Thanks for that, Inder," I said, noticing her smile again. She was the only one among us four who managed to have the friendliness that one would expect from a party of adventurers. "I think I'm good enough to walk, although I might need to be carried if the terrain gets rough or if we have to sprint."

"Abyss needs food to heal from his Diamorph transformations," Diana said. "And more than a standard-sized meal, usually. So as hungry as the three of us might get, we need to feed him first to prevent him from becoming dead weight and to continue his quest."

"Maybe . . . " I called out to the trees. "Nature goddess? Can you drop me another bundle of fruit again? And can the gray cat lead the way through this fog?"

"Nature goddess?" Latis chuckled. "That explains how you were able to survive that foolish jump into the river and how you got all the way here. But if the Witch of the Forest is helping you, if you even managed to make her speak with her human consciousness, then that's another bad sign that we need to avoid."

"Well, I would've probably died of dehydration had she not decided to rain fruit upon me," I said.

"It's a very bad omen," Diana said. "People consider me old at four thousand years, but the Witch of the Forest wants to stretch her roots all the way back to every organism since the Cambrian explosion. Humans and primates are just a blip in time, a puny twig in the tree of life for her."

"We can worry about the Witch of the Forest later," Inder suggested. "We need to either get out of this giant fog cloud or stop it at its origins and seal the crack in space-time."

"And hopefully, since there's the three of you here, I won't have to use my Diamorph transformation as much, and the world stays stable," I said.

Despite their experience, none of my three companions knew which direction to go in, so three kids and one four-thousand-year-old hunter girl continued the adventurer's tradition of walking through the area until something happened. I decided to keep my experience with Simon when I flowed through the quicksilver aether as a secret for now — it hadn't been that eventful in the end, and it could have just been a random dream, after all.

I didn't like breaking or dislocating bones or tearing my muscles every time I used my special power, but besides that, walking alongside Diana, Inder, and Latis in this odd adventure was far more intriguing than anything that I would've experienced if I'd returned to normal life. The three of them all fit the roles in any fantasy story. A skilled archer with a troubled past, an aggressive knife-wielding boy who could move like a ninja, and a friendly ice mage who could perform make-shift medicine.

In the end, I was the odd one out, the hero who only won his battles due to lucky transformations. I would much prefer being a typical sword-wielder with some elemental power to support, or even a mechanical genius, but I suppose that just like in sports, some team members had to play their role. I was definitely just another annoying assigned quest to Latis and Diana, and Oljatu and Grigory's expectations of me were strange, to say the least.

"Did you really mean trying to find a happier ending for me?" Diana asked. I didn't expect her to be so direct about it, especially while Inder and Latis were still marching along.

"I know that Grigory's probably just the tip of the iceberg for this Pharaoh's strategic maneuvers," I said. "And I know real life isn't like in the stories. But do you really think that I could just forget about you after you were the first one to reach out to me after those scrappy first three days at the Western Sanctuary? And Latis didn't help me either when I tried to stand up to Oljatu, so yeah . . ."

"Well, just a heads up. I've had heroes much more intelligent and handsome than you try their best to save me in addition to their quests," Diana said. "And things didn't turn out pretty for them. The heroes I trained that ended up living the longest were the ones that could mostly forget about me. I'm the tragic downfall for failed heroes and the first rung of the ladder for the ones that become legends."

"Fate should never be set in stone like that," I muttered in response.

The ground water flowed through many thin roots, vines, and branches, so thirst wasn't too big of an issue. But when it came to hunger, the party was split as to what we could consider edible food. Inder gestured to the many colorful, patterned mushrooms — some clusters with roofs as wide and round as basketballs — as a potential source of energy, but Diana and Latis vehemently rejected the idea.

"They aren't very nutrient-heavy, for one thing," Diana said. "But the main problem is the mutagenic fog likely brings out the worst in mushrooms. We'll probably hallucinate and kill each other if we even take a small bite of them."

"I can cut out the neurotoxins with my ice magic," Inder insisted. "Although there might be some side effects . . ."

"The best bet has always been to track down animals, carefully gut them, and thoroughly cook them," Latis said. "Although the ground isn't necessarily soft enough for footprints here."

My legs were already beginning to become tired as my bones tried to keep themselves together. "Maybe I could use my sixth sense, just like with the impalas." None of my companions had a problem with that suggestion, but it appeared that I wasn't able to use the power without first confirming a location with my five regular senses. I looked around for disrupted patterns and distortions, as I couldn't rely on my sense of smell or hearing. "Even if the mutagenic fog and my general distortion of space-time made animals much stronger, they still need to regularly feed, right?"

"The gastrointestinal tract is always full whether you cut open an animal or a man," Diana said, agreeing. She seemed to catch my gaze and spoke out on what I was observing. "The bark of the tree trunks in that direction, and the vines and leaves, it looks like they're growing back unevenly. We can follow those patterns instead of using footsteps."

As we followed the trail of disrupted vegetation, I decided to speak about what I had in mind. "If Diana is really immortal, one day humans will evolve enough, either through technology or genetic drift or magic, and what then? I would assume that the two gods who created the universe would still be interested in these Witches and heroes? What constitutes enough mental capacity, enough brain power needed to witness and wield magic?"

"Humans today already look somewhat like a different species," Diana commented. "Taller than they used to be, but also much fatter. Perhaps you herald the cursed future as well as borrowing evolutionary mutations from the past. Maybe the species of the future will both need your sixth sense and your propensity to recklessly charge in."

"I'll try to take that as a compliment," I said. "If that made life less boring and the world more interesting, it'd be pretty cool."

"It's an uphill battle if we take his foolish idealism, as well," Latis said. "In all animals, from insects to deer, aggression gets results when it comes to leaving behind more descendants."

"Quiet down, I heard something," Diana said. She stepped forward silently, readied an arrow, and carefully peered through the fog and vegetation. "Everyone, get ready."

I heard the whiz of Diana's arrow, but no familiar comfortable *thok.* A quadruped with an enormous snout burst out of its cover, and Diana barely rolled aside in time to dodge its strike. Inder luckily had an ice shield ready and stayed by my side to defend me. The creature was probably as heavy as a bull, and Inder's shield cracked from the pressure of the blow, which knocked me over toward the ground. Latis rushed in, his left arm still in a cast, and it seemed like he had a good angle for sure . . .

From what I could see, the hide was too thick, and the strange wild boar swiveled at the perfect timing anyway. It was as if it had been used to dealing with skilled hunters before and knew the basics of human anatomy. My stomach grumbled in despair as Diana let loose another arrow. I could swear that the arrow pierced through the abdomen of the beast, but when I blinked, it was another abrupt change of direction. Hunting this mutated boar, which seemed as if it could read potential predators with the twitching of its nose, was much harder than fighting the buffed impala.

Latis and Diana continued to give chase, but it turned out that the creature's legs were flexible enough to act as hooks as well as hooves. It jumped across the rows of trees and branches, vaulted up like a monkey, and seemed to decide to wait for the next move.

"Maybe we should just look for grubs feeding on rotten wood again?" I suggested.

The agile mutant boar wasn't fleeing from us, however. It was gazing at each of us with its beady eyes, and its snout still twitched as if it wanted something particular. We were more than predators—did this creature want our clothes, our brains, or some way to steal our magic power?

"The mutagenic fog is pretty powerful to create a creature that could dodge my arrows twice," Diana said.

"What if it's not dodging the arrows?" I asked. "What if it already knew where your arrows were going?"

"If it could read the future, it would have just fled instead of allowing me to stalk it," Diana answered. "Unless it was protecting its territory or young . . . hmm. Maybe we really do need to just go for smaller targets, even if they make smaller meals."

"*Hrrrhrrnk.*" I tried to do the best pig impression I could do. I sort of wanted this creature to suddenly speak English, but I was just given more snorting.

Is it some sort of echolocation, like a bat, whale, or dolphin? Human beings required expensive equipment and software in order to emulate Mother Nature, but if my Diamorph powers could even get a glimpse of it . . .

"It might be stuck in a certain spherical section of space once it activated its power to read the future."

"Looks like you're our best bet for some meat then, Abyss," Latis said. "Why don't you sprout a piggy snout?"

As I closed my eyes, I tried to imagine myself in this weird boar's position. All stimuli came from the very recent past through the reflection of electromagnetic waves. The future could only be predicted through previous experience and knowledge of physics with body coordination. If human thought processes were predictable enough for just several seconds in advance, and if this creature's echolocation instantly communicated future movements . . .

As I snorted, I *felt* two waves of stimuli cancel themselves out in front of me. The boar-like creature no longer had my thoughts in mind, and it seemed to panic. I would have to make the killing blow, but I still moved too slowly, and it could just be avoided. "Throw a knife, Latis. And Diana, imagine that you're shooting, but fire one second *after* I command you to."

Diana nodded silently, as if trying not to alert the boar of our plan. Latis tossed a knife in the mutant boar's direction, and as the boar scrambled about, I could see the trails of echolocation, which read Diana's intent to fire on command. I was still able to somewhat cancel out the thought wave that it had gathered from me, and as the creature decelerated as it landed on a lower branch, I knew that this was our opportunity.

"Fire!" I yelled, and the mutant boar darted back, sure that it had successfully dodged a ready arrow. Diana did her best to act frustrated, her arrow still ready as she waited for the creature to helplessly fly through the air, obedient to inertia and general physics.

Thok.

The arrow shaft spurted out from the boar's side, but it had somehow still managed to twist its body just enough to protect its vital organs. It landed as swiftly as a cat and charged down the obvious target—me. Diana was still re-loading her arrows, and Latis was reaching for his knife when my left leg was tackled by its charge, sending me toppling over like a clumsy fool. When I landed on the hard ground, I realized that my echolocation ability had dissipated, my ears rattled by the sudden shock.

"Don't worry," Inder said as she grabbed one of my arms and helped me to my feet. "I can track down the blood trail, no matter how slight, with my magic." Inder froze the ground underneath her, felt the ice for discrepancies, and directed our party of four toward our escaping prey. Inder tried to chill some of my bruised muscles with her magic, but I was still stumbling and trailing behind Diana and Latis.

"The ones with the most useful abilities have to be the slowest, huh?" Latis grumbled as he pressed Inder for directions.

"I wish we could all live on a ship and just have whatever food served to us," I said. "We won't have to run into another group trying to steal our kill, will we?" All of this seemed awfully repetitive, even if I was beginning to gain new powers. I would prefer a cheesy and incompetent villain from children's books, even though those were irritating to read about.

"Ants," Inder noticed as she continued to follow the blood trail. "Lots of them."

"By chance, they aren't humongous ones that will impale us on their limbs?"

"The laws of physics aren't warped that much, you know," Diana said. "A huge ant would either have a hollowed-out inside or would collapse under its own weight." I was relieved that I wouldn't have to face any enormous insect monsters or just wondered if they would have the exoskeleton on their body with muscular, mammal-like limbs.

"We'll be lucky if half of the meat is still there," Latis said. "Mutant ants are no bigger than normal ones, but they work five to ten times faster." Latis took a bottle of chemicals from his half-sister and now could spot the trail of ants with his bare eyes and tracked down the swarming creatures as their ranks thickened. I saw that Latis breathed a sigh of relief after spilling the chemicals across the black swarm.

"They do work fast, all right . . . " My eyes widened as I saw the results. Around sixty percent of the mutant boar had been stripped clean to its bone, exposing its entire skull, rib cage, and front two limbs. I wasn't sure if the bottom half was all right to eat, given that the body had been riddled with ant bites, but like always, I didn't have room to be picky.

Inder carefully observed the half-eaten body and doused it with more of her special chemicals. "He's edible, but it's difficult to access bone marrow when it comes to these mutated animals. We might draw some attention from creatures with the fire, but bacteria strains get wilder outside of the mortal world, so everything has to be cooked thoroughly."

"I thought most animals were afraid of the fire," I said. "Although I suppose the fire-spitting monsters are staples of fantasy as well, right? That doesn't violate the laws of physics the same way insect legs work on a man-sized beast." Diana still appeared to find my questions annoying, but she seemed a bit less annoyed than usual. "I wonder if the possibilities for my Diamorph powers are indeed limitless," I said. "So far, I don't think using the boar's echolocation is cursing me too much . . ."

"All Witches have their respected curses," Diana said. "Whether it comes in the near or far future varies, perhaps just for a twist. Perhaps the only reason I was given immortality was because I'm waiting for a curse." I wasn't sure if she was serious about the suggestion, and Latis chipped in on the conversation.

"They aren't limitless in the fact that no one who started as a mortal lifeform, or even a computer-generated program for that matter . . . none of us will reach the primordial essences of the two gods, of order and chaos. Things aren't like in mythology, where Cronos could butcher Uranus, and Zeus could then rebel against Cronos," Latis said. "But who knows? Perhaps in a galaxy far away, lizard-men conceal their existence and watch us like scientists study lab rats."

But even with those limitations, factions, from Melosh's priests to the ancient Pharaoh to the Witch of the Forest, all had tried to change the world for better, whatever that meant. However, I was only a thirteen-year-old boy with all of the expected limitations. When I thought of being a hero, all I could do was clumsily and recklessly charge in and try to save people, much to Latis and Diana's chagrin. Diana carefully dried the bow and spinner she used with her animal pelts, and Inder chipped in to make the site of the fire as dry as possible. The mutagenic mist made everything more difficult, and I could see the sweat and frustration on the cheetah-cheeked hunter.

"Couldn't we manage to gather flints or create a box of matches with chemicals?" I asked. "Or even carry a handheld gas-lighter? It seems strange that we were never given such things on our adventures."

"Using short-cuts is a sure way to get on the God of Fire's wrong side," Latis said. "Heck, a lot of people rumor that the God of Fire generally disapproves of any technology past the twentieth century." Diana ground through her frustration and eventually got an ember, placed it into the stash of dry leaves, and blew carefully.

"But . . . if he really has such a sentiment, why didn't he stop human evolution mid-way and just force our kind to return to monkeys?" I asked. "Using fire was a cheat code in itself, since it allowed us to increase caloric density, soften food, and even improve our current tools to some extent."

Latis shrugged. "Perhaps we humans were too strange that he had no choice but to let us continue to pillage and prosper in order to satisfy his need for entertainment."

My stomach continued to grumble once the butchered meat was placed over the open fire. I was glad that I was finally given a chance to relax ever since I'd been forced into training by Oljatu, but at the same time, none of the world seemed to make any sense. But perhaps it was the same thing for scientists every time microscopes and particle accelerators became more powerful. Answering questions only led to more mysteries and concepts. "We probably won't have any of it to preserve, given your usual appetite increase whenever you transform," Diana admitted.

"Well, we have somewhat of a strategy for hunting down similar creatures," I said. "Or will mutations happen so fast for the animals here that I won't be able to keep up?"

Diana poked and prodded at the meat to see if it was tender. "Maybe you could use your ability to either climb high up into the trees or go underground. But both areas are pretty dangerous, and if you transformed yourself for mobility, you probably wouldn't have the needed fighting prowess."

I tried to counter Diana, but I remembered how pathetic I'd looked in most of my battles. Even in the ones I'd managed to win, I was bruised purple and hardly surviving at the end of the day.

"Then let's just hope my body memorizes the past-future echolocation skill," I said. "If I can carve out a feasible future that way, right?"

"It's too bad the brain was completely eaten by the ants,"

Latis chipped in. "But maybe you can increase some of your agility by eating one of its legs?" Diana handed me my section of the mutant boar, which was the enormous leg and thigh piece. It should have been more than enough for a kid of my height and weight, but I had to restore quite an amount of body mass from the fight with Grigory and then the hunt itself. I didn't even think much about how the flesh tasted as I tore into the light brown muscles and probably didn't chew enough as the meat went down my throat.

"Well, if you're not as lucky as a cartoon character, you're certainly as boorish as one when it comes to eating," Latis commented between bites of his strips of flesh. I was pretty reckless in my quest to feed my stomach, and when I bit down on the hard bone, even Diana managed to giggle a little. She really was cute when she smiled, even if she didn't have the grace of a despondent princess.

"I'm all right," I said. My gums were bleeding a little, but my teeth were still in place. "Maybe I could eventually invest in some crocodile teeth as well . . . " Diana's face grew stern all of a sudden. "Was it a bad joke?"

"Abyss!" Latis said as he tackled me. An enormous, hippo-like creature with chitin armor bowled through our campsite, and I quickly realized it wasn't alone. "Run for it!" Latis said as he rolled away.

As I made a lucky dodge, my shoulder was jostled just enough by the slight contact, forcing me to drop the leg meat. I wanted to finish my meal, but I also knew that I had to survive. My stomach was still rumbling as I saw Inder slide through the rampaging herd on a frozen sheet of icy dirt. Latis and Diana were nowhere in sight, but I could hear their shouts and battle cries.

Inder was sliding in the wrong direction while she clumsily toggled her ice magic—if I didn't divert her path, she would be quickly trampled by the next hippo. I bolted forward, went into a dive, and used the slippery icy floor. I could only grab onto her arm and divert her direction a little as I forced her in my direction, and I watched as the hippo's legs skimmed her blue hair. I had almost been too late, but . . .

"Watch out below!" Inder warned as the two of us tumbled through a rather steep hill. I hadn't seen any of the geography in the thick fog, and as Inder and I took turns crashing our backs into the hard dirt, I desperately tried to grab whatever ledge I could find with my free hand.

To be continued . . .

ABOUT THE AUTHOR

Andy Hsieh is a sci-fi and fantasy enthusiast. Although his first passion is creative writing, he also creates animations, illustrations, and independent video games, and is always eager to experiment with and explore new ideas. After starting his initial attempts at writing fiction in middle school, he has retained a strong interest in the stories of antiheroes and villains, peculiar philosophical conundrums, and epic quests for adventure. Throughout many trials, tribulations, and incomplete projects, he found the determination to push on and improve through many years of raw experience. Hsieh graduated with his B.A. in Philosophy, Law and Society in 2017, and currently resides in Northern California.

www.ingramcontent.com/pod-product-compliance
Lightning Source LLC
Chambersburg PA
CBHW060833120626
46557CB00001B/487